The Ways' Favorite

WYNN STEVENSON

ISBN 978-1-7361332-2-4 (paperback)
ISBN 978-1-7361332-3-1 (eBook)

Printed in the United States of America

CONTENTS

AUTHOR'S NOTE

I wrote a large portion of this book while listening to a selection of songs provided to me by Pandora. Certain songs seemed to resonate with the storyline. You may find all four of the songs on YouTube by either typing in the name of the song and artist in the search box or clicking on the hyperlink provided. If the latter, you may have to hold down the "CRTL" key while clicking on the link. While you may have to listen to a few commercials, I think the music adds to what I hope you find an enjoyable escape.

Chapter/Song title by Artist
Prologue* <u>Beyond</u> by William Joseph
5A <u>The Heart Asks Pleasure First</u> by Myleene Klaus
5B <u>Italian Summer</u> by Brian Crain
20* <u>Made to Love You</u> by Toby Mac

PROLOGUE

Music (Beyond by William Joseph) https://www.youtube.com/watch?v=hrqMgYovGJ0

The Raven was tired of being disguised as a pigeon. He longed to get back in his body and soar with the wind. Use his extraordinarily long tail feathers, which only ravens could properly display, and ride the currents away from this wretched city. Away from the city that had entrapped his master these past forty years. Trapped in a horrible curse that kept him from functioning, from knowing who he was. A curse that would have defeated any other soul. However, if master weren't dead, he may as well have been these past forty years.

The Raven-disguised-as-a-pigeon nodded his head and hopped over to the ledge. Perhaps the red man was right. Perhaps this time they would break through. Yet, the red man could come up with some extraordinarily stupid plans. This one had taken root almost twenty years ago. At first the Raven thought that there was no way the plan would ever be needed. Then he thought the plan would never work. Now he realized it was their last hope.

They had tried on numerous occasions, so many attempts, yet nothing seemed to work. His master still came to this bookstore every morning at the break of day not to leave until the streets were dark. Even the old and the wise had all failed. Only today, maybe today would see an end to the torment.

It had been a cold and rainy early January day in the city. Now as evening approached, it seemed the temperature took a much more significant plunge than was warranted. The Raven-disguised-as-a-pigeon flew down to the cellar window to get a better look inside only to have his feet greeted by the cool water that had accumulated on the cement ledge throughout the day. The red man said to stay away, but what could it hurt? If they knew it was him, he would already be dead. As he arrived on his cold wet perch a girl, the-most-beautiful-girl-the-Raven-had-ever-seen, walked down the steps and went behind the shelves of books into the Physics and Engineering textbooks. Just as planned, she emerged with a single volume of *Introduction to Thermal Physics* by Dr. Solomon Horowitz. The Raven-disguised-as-a-pigeon hopped from foot-to-foot and smiled, his plan was working!

"Excuse me," said the-most-beautiful-girl-the-Raven-had-ever-seen. "Do you know if this is the text required by Professor Horowitz for this coming semmester's class, number 800?"

The man behind the information desk, his master, looked up from the newspaper he had been reading. He was a man that appeared to be in his mid-twenties. He had sandy colored hair cut short but in need of a trim. His eyes, though a deep blue seemed cloudy as if coming off a long night's binge. He wore an untucked New York Mets jersey with blue pinstripes. Over the right pocket was the team logo, and on the back of the jersey where you would normally find the player's name, was the word Metz. His master reached for the book, and as the Raven-disguised-as-a-pigeon looked on through the barred window in uncontainable anticipation, it happened!

The clerk's and the-most-beautiful-girl-the-Raven-had-ever-seen eyes met for the first time. The inquiring student stood about five-foot eight with an athletic build and long ash blonde hair held back in a ponytail. Her eyes were green. They were not bluish-green or sea colored green, but a strange surreal emerald. As their eyes locked and their hands touched, on the part of the book they each held, it seemed as though the book itself emitted sparks. The sparks sprung out of the book in a glorious rainbow of colors. Upon this event several things happened simultaneously, most notably all the power in the building went out. Milliseconds after the power went out all the light from whatever origin was sucked out of the building. Not only the rainbow of light emitted from the book, but all light, cell phones, emergency lights and even the light reflected into the bookstore from the neon sign across the street. Many of the patrons in the store, let out at a scream. It was pitch black. In addition, there was a definite smell of sulfur in the air. Many of those inside the building at the time assumed, incorrectly, the smell was the result of some burning wires.

The young student intent on purchasing the text thought she saw a spark, but felt little of the associated energy surge. As she took a step back, she heard a voice above the screams asking for everyone to stay calm. The voice, from the security staff member, told everyone that it was just a power shortage. The whole block was out, but everyone was safe. After several minutes, the emergency lights and the flashlights from cell phones were able to run and everyone worked their way to the exit on the principal level. Soon everyone, including the most-beautiful-girl-the-Raven-had-ever-seen had escaped the building. Everyone that is except the information clerk with the Mets jersey. He was face down and unconscious.

The Raven-disguised-as-a-pigeon continued to hop from foot to foot in relief and anxiety. Relief for what had finally happened and in anxiety for what was to come. If pigeons could smile, one formed on the bird's bill. He knew it had worked! His plan worked flawlessly. It only took another pair of emerald green eyes.

Just then a female clerk that had come out of the bookstore gave a loud screech of what sounded like, "Abschaum! (*Scum*)" and directed a quick kick in the direction of the Raven-disguised-as-a-pigeon. He hopped away from the window and took flight. It was too dangerous to stay any longer, even disguised as a pigeon.

chapter 1

JOHN

"Mr. Metz, please come in," said Jason Dowdy the recently appointed proud new manager of the Barnes and Noble Columbia University Bookstore at 2922 Broadway in New York City. He tried to put on a welcoming face. The fore mentioned Mr. Metz a youngish almost professorial looking candidate sat down in a blue leather winged back chair opposite Mr. Dowdy.

"Mr. Metz, you probably already know our chief-of-security Mr. Homes," He nodded toward a stocky gentleman with a military crew cut and a guarded military bearing. Mr. Homes in return nodded toward the newly arrived meeting participant. His look portrayed a mixture of curiosity and loathing.

"And this gentleman you probably have discovered lurking in your neck of the woods, the textbook section, is Dr. Solomon Horowitz," added Mr. Dowdy nodding to a distinguished looking man. Dr. Horowitz wore his camel hair jacket and blue jeans as a symbol of his intelligence. Combine the camel hair jacket with dark brown patches at the elbows, his wispy white hair in need of a haircut and the bifocals that he never used, but hung around his neck on a silver chain, made him somebody who would never be mistaken for anything other than a

Physics Professor. The Professor smiled at Mr. Metz, as if he was slightly ashamed for dragging him before a congressional hearing chaired by the opposition party.

"Now then," began Mr. Dowdy a meticulously dressed man in his late forties. Comfortable in his bow tie and his new found authority. Even though he did not need them, he peered out over the top of his cropped glasses. "It is Metz, isn't it?" asked the bookstore manager.

"John will do," replied the wrongly addressed Mr. Metz. John was someone to whom you would never pay much attention. While sitting in the blue leather winged backed chair, he all but disappeared. He was wearing an old blue pin stripped Mets jersey, worn denim jeans and comfortable, but also well-worn leather shoes. His washed out brown hair was neat, but it was obvious he needed a haircut. His eyes appeared blue, but very dull. He looked to be in his early twenties, but who could say. Who could say indeed?

Mr. Dowdy hesitated, looked toward Mr. Homes, cleared his throat then continued, "Yes. Well, John that demonstrates one of the problems quite frankly. You may appreciate I've only been on the job for about a month. So, I can't have been expected to have had the time to meet all fifty-five of our associates. John I'll be blunt, from what we can tell you've worked here for close to forty years and we have no record of who you are or that you've ever received a paycheck."

Professor Horowitz looked shocked. Clearly the man before him was no older than many of his graduate students. Even so, how does one work in a place for forty years and nobody know his name? Not to mention survive in this city without a paycheck?

"Mr. Homes perhaps you can repeat for the Professor what you and I discussed earlier today. Maybe John can even fill-in some of the missing information," suggested Mr. Dowdy.

Mr. Homes cleared his throat, "Well, yes, as Mr. Dowdy knows I've only been on the job a bit longer than he has," already offering up an excuse. "In fact, the turnover at this particular location has been extremely high with the exception of Mr. Mmm, John." Mr. Homes corrected his use of the name Metz which was obviously in error.

Mr. Homes continued, "From what I've been able to uncover, John has been with us since 1981. I was able to get in touch with several former employees and store managers, including, a Mr. Herman Frank, who managed the store when it was owned by the University. He's retired now, but he was shocked to hear Mr. Metz (a slip) was still here. He claimed John here just showed up one morning and started working at the textbook information desk. He said and I quote, He had an amazing aptitude for Physics and was very helpful to all the students."

Mr. Homes stared at the man before him as if in disbelief at his own research notes, "He, Mr. Frank, said he remembered him as if it was yesterday, I quote, he was wearing a Mets jersey and he wore it every day. Everyone just took up calling him Mr. Metz. The peculiar thing was we never put him on the payroll yet he never missed a day of work and we never had any complaints. Not a one!"

All three men in the room stared at John, who seemed relaxed as if he wasn't even in the room. "In fact," continued Mr. Homes his voice breaking, "I was able to contact six of the twenty-one store managers who have managed this store since 1981. All six said they remembered Mr. Metz but no one knew anything about him except he was courteous, easy going and was never added to the staff." At the conclusion of Mr. Homes reading his notes a silence fell over the room.

"Yes. Well, John, you begin to see our befuddlement. You seem to have outlasted everyone who works here by decades. You never miss a day of work. In fact, Mr. Homes searched back through the security camera database and it appears you have not missed a day of work, seven days a week, for as far back as the tapes are available, sixty days. Further, you've never been on the payroll." Mr. Dowdy finished as if he expected John to provide some kind of explanation. When none was forthcoming, he cleared his throat "well..." he said staring at John over the top of his glasses.

"Obviously there's been a mistake," said John. At this, all three men looked relieved. "It wasn't that long and I like it here, why should I be paid for something I enjoy."

"John, while it's obvious you couldn't have been here since 1981." He rolled his eyes at Mr. Homes whom he now considered inept. "Can you at least tell us a bit about yourself? Maybe we can start with your full name."

John hesitated a few seconds and let out a long sigh, "Well, there's not much to tell, my name is John Newton."

Professor Horowitz sucked is his breath, "Excuse me," he stated.

Mr. Homes interjected hopefully, "You know him Professor?"

"No, sorry for interrupting Mr. Newton" said the Professor. "Please continue."

"Well, I love working in the stacks downstairs and I love helping the students here at Columbia University," said John.

Mr. Dowdy looked at his watch, this whole meeting was ridiculous and obviously a waste of his valuable time. The kid looked no more than twenty-five and it appeared he was not going to provide any information. As far as he was concerned if the kid wanted to work for free who cared what his name was anyhow. "Yes, well, we can sort some of this paperwork out later, after the Professor leaves." Mr. Dowdy cleared his throat, "Professor, you're the one who brought all this to a head. Perhaps you should present to Mr. Newton what you showed me yesterday."

The Professor reached into his briefcase and withdrew a thick seven hundred plus page textbook. "Have you ever seen this book Mr. Newton?" asked the Professor handing over the book to the young man.

John accepted the book and thumbed through it. He smiled, handing the heavy book back to the Professor. "So you're the young man who wrote the book an *Introduction to Thermal Physics*. Nice to meet you, Professor. However, other than helping your students carry that book to the cashier, I can't say that I'm familiar with it," said John.

The Professor accepted the book back from John and smiled. He caught John referring to him as a young man and he incorrectly assumed he was being teased, as being someone older than John himself. "Yes, it's a bit weighty especially in this age of eBooks. But...," the Professor looked into John's dull eyes and said, "But this book is unique. It has all the answers to all the problems written out in a very strong hand. All of them are in ink and all of them appear to be absolutely correct."

"You have some very good students," smiled John, who for the first time had a bit of a gleam in his eyes.

The Professor continued, "Not only are all the answers correct. The person writing in the book corrected fifty-three unique formulas. Formulas, I might add that are all accepted as fact and yet I see the hand of a genius in these corrections. In particular," said the professor flying to a page that had been marked with a red ribbon, "In the back, here, this correction on page six hundred and eighty-three."

The Professor handed the book back over to John, who looked down at the book he had carelessly corrected. As John looked down at his hand writing the Professor continued, "From Newton's *Principia*, it's the law of universal gravitation. Every particle in the universe is attracted to every other particle by a force proportional to a product of their masses and inversely proportional to the square of the distance between them."

$$F = G\frac{m_1 m_2}{r^2}$$

The formula above was displayed in the text as part of the footnotes. However, written alongside the formula in the same hand that had written throughout the text was:

$$F = ((Gm1/m2)/r^2)\ (A+\Omega+\psi)^{\ 3}$$

The Professor wet his lips as if expecting the opening of the skies. "What is alpha-omega-psi cubed Mr. Newton?" The Professor sucked in his breath in shock as he looked into the now sparkling blue eyes of John Newton. Eyes that were no longer dull blue, but an ocean in turmoil.

"What does your soul tell you Saul?" asked John.

Professor Horowitz was taken aback by the use of his nickname and he shook his head not understanding the question. He could only look imploringly into John's eyes.

"Saul, if you were meant to know you would already recognize the truth. I'm sorry, I can't tell you," said John.

"You can't or you won't," begged the Professor.

"I guess it's one in the same Saul," John answered.

The professor leaned back defeated, but made one last attempt, "I had hoped to keep her out of this."

"Her?" asked John the bemused smile vanishing instantly.

"Yes," said the Professor seeing he was right all along, right about everything. "My young student who allowed me to borrow this book after I saw her referring to it in my class." The Professor could tell he had John's full attention, no more games. "She mentioned she had bought the book here. She said when she first picked-it out, before this semester began, there was an incident which stopped her from making the purchase. When she came back and retrieved it, it was... well, what student can refuse a complete set of answers."

"I'm sorry, but like I said Professor, I can't help you," said John the gleam in his eyes all but disappearing.

The Professor ignored John's rebuff and continued, "When I inquired about what sort of incident. She said when she first came to this bookstore, she went to ask at the information desk if she had the right textbook for Thermodynamics 800. Just as the handsome young man and she touched hands, as they exchanged the book, there was a spark. She stated it was very surreal as all the light in the building seemed to evaporate. It was as if all the light was sucked out of the building. Even the cell phones didn't work. Of course, at the time I didn't believe her." The Professor paused and then added softly, "Of course, I do now."

The Professor looked over at Mr. Homes and Mr. Dowdy only to be shocked as both men seemed completely frozen their faces staring blankly into space. Despite the fact that he suspected this was soon to be his fate, he asked calmly, "Who are you?" Then added hesitantly in a soft voice, "What are you?"

John vacillated and then stood up and went over to the window and adjusted the blinds so they opened slightly. He peered out the window to the street below, then turned back to the Professor, "How's the young lady? Is she in trouble?" asked John.

"Trouble from me, of course not," the Professor regretted saying this as John was obviously not referring to him as a possible source of trouble. "She is as beautiful as she is brilliant, a tremendous diamond in the rough. No one would hurt her." He paused, "But now that you mention it. Yes, but, yes Mr. Newton the truth is I think she is in some kind of difficulty. Since I borrowed this book, Alexandra, Ms. Holt, has not been to class. In fact, I went to the Dean earlier this week and I encouraged them to start an inquiry as to her whereabouts. But the University's security is even worse than this book store's. That's when I resolved to look into this on my own." said the Professor. "As I suspected when I saw a four hundred year old formula altered by an obvious genius, I knew there had to be forces involved beyond my imagination, beyond my comprehension," he said this as he looked at the two paralyzed meeting participants.

"They're fine," said John. "I, just can't have many people being made aware that I've woken up. I'm not strong enough yet." He said this as he closed the blinds after once again looking narrowly out on Broadway Avenue.

"Not strong enough? Awoken? What does this all mean? See here, I came about the book, but if Ms. Holt is in danger and you're involved I have to report this to the authorities. I can see now Ms. Holt is in peril. I have to..." said the Professor as his eyes glazed over and he froze in place the same as Mr. Dowdy and Mr. Homes.

"Sorry Doc," said John to himself. "I'm sure you mean well, but you just don't realize what you're up against, what we're up against."

John turned and nervously checked out the window one last time. He looked at his ancient wrist watch, took the book from the Professor's lap, and with a nod made the book disappear. It just vanished. John sat back down in the blue leather winged back chair and made sure everything was as it had been when he and Solomon started to discuss the book. Checked his watch one more time and then clicked his fingers.

Mr. Dowdy cleared his throat, "Professor, you're the one who brought all this to a head. Perhaps you should present to Mr. Metz what you showed me yesterday."

The Professor reached into his briefcase and started thumbing through a series of papers. "I apologize," said the Professor. "I thought I had a book with me. An amazing book really." He continued to look down into his briefcase as all three men watched him fumble with its contents. "I just don't know what may have happened to it," he whispered.

"Well, can you tell us about it Professor?" asked the security chief impatiently but obviously amused.

"I, well, yes, I..." but the Professor seemed to lose his train of thought. He looked completely confounded his eyes out of focus.

"Yes, well," said Mr. Dowdy with eyes as glazed over as the Professor's. "Without the book I see no reason for us to keep Mr. Metz away from his work."

John rose out of his chair and shook the hands of Mr. Dowdy and Mr. Homes. When he came over to stand in front of the Professor, the poor man was still bent over, fumbling with the contents of his briefcase. John's eyes had turned back to their dowdy shade of blue.

"Professor Horowitz, it was a pleasure meeting you," said Mr. Metz extending his hand.

"Yes, delightful, meeting you Mr. Metz," said the flummoxed Professor still looking for the non-existent book.

John Newton left the office and closed the door. The seven hundred page love letter he had so carelessly and recently written was shrunken and tucked into his back pocket.

chapter 2

REMY

The subway car rattled along through the night. It was on these trains where John spent his nights when he was not serving students at the Columbia University bookstore. The nearest station to the bookstore was Van Cortland Park at 242nd street directly across from Broadway Joe's Pizza. The walk of five blocks to the station seemed different to John this evening. He had walked the path so many nights in a fog that it wasn't until these past few days that he even noticed the array of food shops within the community he had taken for granted these past forty years. He had questioned himself earlier that evening, as he walked past the entrance to Van Cortland Park, how many of the businesses had even been there when he was first incarcerated.

As he took his seat he was put off by the uncleanliness of the commuter train. That was one thing about being in a fog the past forty years, nothing had seemed to matter, now he felt a bit claustrophobic and almost nauseous. The train was noisy, and smelled which was the norm, but tonight it seemed even more congested and foul than usual. It had been a full week since he had met with Dowdy, Homes and Horowitz. As he had expected, nothing had come of it. The spell which had been woven around him had made him essentially invisible to the store's

10

administration. He had been concerned that there would be some form of follow-up forcing him to depart before he had time to heal, but thus far not even the Professor had bothered him. He was extremely worried about the girl, but at this point he wasn't even sure who she was or how she came to be in the bookstore. The Professor had called her Alexandra Holt, the first name brought back haunting memories, but he didn't recognize the last name. Their coming together had been very brief, just a fleeting touch really. Yet, something had definitely happened when they touched, but whether it was the spell finally wearing off or the touch of the girl herself John had no way of knowing. Until...

"Don't turn around, I may have been followed," said Professor Horowitz in a soft shaky whisper.

John's shoulders slumped, the Professor would not have been followed because John was rarely if ever left alone. In fact, ever since the incident with the girl, John had noticed that the number of guards around him were increasing almost on a daily basis. It was as if they were waiting for John to make a break for it, but didn't want to interpose if the curse was still working.

John got up and moved away heading toward and into the next car, hoping the Professor would get the hint and not follow him. Unfortunately, it was not to be.

"Mr. Metz, please we have to speak," hissed the Professor as he and John entered the next car.

John turned to look at the man and was shocked at what he saw, he thought he was looking at a derelict. They had met just a week ago, but the Professor looked ashen and frightened. His once natty exterior was dirty, torn and disheveled.

"Mr. Metz, please it's my student the one to whom you gave the book. She's still missing and I think you know who may have taken her.

I'm very worried her..." He trailed off as three men suddenly surrounded him and John. To say they were huge would have provided the bare minimum of the description. They could hardly stand up straight in the subway car. They seemed to have suffered some serious wounds, but whoever in their right mind would have challenged these thugs to inflict such wounds was beyond the realm of logic.

"I tried to tell you Professor," sighed John. "I'm not strong enough yet."

Suddenly, everything in the car became still. The ceaseless rocking of the subway car stopped. A chill descended throughout the car. Every person on the train except for John, the Professor and the three huge men were frozen in time. Suddenly, there was a not so subtle shaking of the car in which they were standing when the train door opened, despite there not being a subway stop nearby, and in walked a hideous, vile humpbacked man dragging a putrid woman by her long filthy hair onto the car.

"Is this who you were worried about Professor?" asked the squat troll of a man. If the act of dragging the girl by the hair had not made him ugly. His appearance would have drawn one to the same conclusion. His face was scarred with a nameless disease. Boils on his face oozed a yellow, sickly puss that would not be stopped. His hair looked as if he had recently undergone chemotherapy. His clothes seemed as if they had never been washed and to say his smell was sulfurous insulted the chemical.

"No," gasped the Professor. He instinctively moved toward his student only to be punched in the solar plexus and dropped immediately to his knees gasping for air.

"Please," screamed the girl, "Please, I'm begging you. I need the shot. I'll do anything you want. You know I'll do anything. Just give me the scat."

John flinched, but didn't move. The girl, Alexandra, was covered in filth, much of it her own. Despite the cold, damp January winter weather she wore no coat. Her clothes were torn and hung limply on her body. She wore no shoes or socks and as a result her feet were almost black. Her once beautiful blonde hair was matted with vomit.

"Now, now Darl'n. I said I'd give you a shot, but only if you behaved," the ogre of a man smiled and revealed a mouth of broken and rotted teeth. He showed the begging girl a syringe full of liquid which he had pulled from his pocket. "How' bout you give old Remy a kiss?"

The girl didn't hesitate, she immediately jumped up, put her arms around the troll's neck and started licking the boils on his face. She put her tongue into his sulphureous mouth. After a few seconds the man pushed her to the floor, putting the syringe back in his pocket. The three men surrounding John and the Professor laughed and taunted vexatiously.

She fell away but began to squeal, "You promised, you promised, I need a fix." She reached out to grab at the troll's pocket only to have her sobs for a fix met by a vicious backhand that tossed her head into a stout metal pole that left her unconscious.

"What have you done to her!" screamed the Professor who had risen to all fours. His rage and consciousness was short lived as he was struck prostrate to the ground by a viscous kick to his groin.

"Well, Johnny. I have you to thank for this tasty morsel," said Remy. "After watching you rot for the last forty years she's been a well-deserved treat." Remy smiled again. "What nothing to say Johnny? Ready to go back to your tomb?" Remy's laugh sounded more like a wheeze from the air filtering through his rotted teeth. The other three men joined their boss in a moment of mirth. They had been concerned when they were assigned the task of going to pick-up John. They had heard so many stories about him. How strong he'd been. Now all they could see was a defeated and weak target. They had all three been bullies growing up and they enjoyed nothing more than beating a weak human being incapable of putting up a defense.

The Professor, on the other hand, who had just barely regained consciousness was used to being obeyed. He was used to being respected and protected by those around him. He rose to his knees with tears, "My god, what have they done to you?" cried the Doctor in defeat. He was able to find where they had taken Alexandra after going undercover as a homeless man. Once he located her he tried going to the police, but as he reached to open the police station door just last night, he was intercepted by the three men that confronted him now. He was badly beaten and warned that if he tried to go to the police again he would be killed. Mr. Metz had been his last hope. He made a move to crawl over to the girl only to have his head pulled back by his hair and a knife brought to his throat.

"Quite you. No use wasting what little time you've left worry'n bout others. We warned you to stay out of this," said the man with the knife.

It was at this point, with their attention distracted by the Professor that John bent down and gently dragged Alexandra's torn sleeve back up her arm. It was covered with needle tracks. Dozens and dozens up both her arms. "What drug did you use?" asked John barely audible.

"Well, not that it matters much to either of you," said Remy in an almost human voice. "It was a simple heroin mixture. We actually had very few questions for her, but she was more than willing." Remy, smiled a wicked grin. "More than willing, Johnny."

"Why so much?" asked John in a scarcely audible voice.

"She kept asking for more, Johnny. Gottfried gave her to me to use as I please. Gottfried said it was my reward for years of valuable service," growled the troll.

"Did he now? Gottfried actually knows your name? You must be moving up in the world Remy," taunted John.

The ogre's grin didn't diminish, "You're the one going back to a tomb. Always so proud, so cocky. After I'm done with er, er and the kindly professor, they'll be found in an abandoned railcar. Imagine what the newspapers will say about em." Remy gave out a raspy imitation of a laugh joined once again by his companions.

"No, that's not what their future holds," said John.

What happened next shocked the Professor even more than seeing Alexandra in such a horrible state. While John still bent over the unconscious girl, the guard with the knife turned and slashed his two comrades across their throats. Blood gushed out everywhere and covered the Professor and John's back as he shielded the girl from being splattered with blood.

Before Remy could raise a cry the knife wielder slit his own throat with such force that he actually removed his own head. It was the head falling into Remy's hands that spurred Remy to action. He threw the head aside and swept his body toward John picking him up with his blood covered hands clamped around John's throat.

"How dare you! How dare you!" He cried as tried to collapse John's throat. "I'll crush you! I'll crush you!" Remy screamed.

Remy's cries of outrage were soon replaced with his squeals of pain. Blood gushed out of his eye socket from where a syringe full of heroin had been plunged into his eye by the still comatose Alexandra. The ogre slumped to the floor of the subway car now covered in blood, some of it his own. John made a movement with his right hand and the knife flew from the floor near the three bodies into his hand. John placed the knife in the now unconscious ogre's blood soaked hand. The authorities can sort out what happened thought John. I don't have the energy left to clean this up.

As he looked around and assured himself that time was still frozen. John walked over to Alexandra, who was standing, but still unconscious. Her head sagged down to her shoulder. John had used her to take out her tormentor. It was poetic justice thought John. He gave her a hug and kissed her on the cheek. He whispered a few words and she collapsed into his arms. As John held her, he noted she weighed so little it was as if he was only holding a bundle of rags.

He turned to the Professor, who was in shock, but realized he should be thankful for being alive. A kind of lavender mist seemed to come along out of nowhere at first surrounding him and then sticking to his skin. He instantly felt calm. His recent injuries and previously broken ribs somehow seemed to heal. His ashen pallor was washed away with what felt like a gentle hand. "I can't hold this entire train in suspension much longer. This scuffle has taken all my reserves. I suspect that only Remy's taunts allowed me enough adrenaline to buy us our freedom," said John in an amazingly calm voice.

The Professor regaining some of his faculties stood up and asked, "How? How did you manage.., who were these men? You killed four men in seconds." The Professor was not sure of whom he should be more afraid. What John had done was not humanly possible.

"No," said John with conviction, "I killed no one. The three deceased men hated each other and even themselves. I merely released their inhibitions. I brought no weapon to this meeting Doctor. In any case, we've no time to argue the fine points. You have to run and you have to hide. Don't go back to the school. Don't go back to your past. You're in more danger than you can possibly imagine. I'll contact you when it's safe. Until you hear from me, or Ms. Holt stay hidden," said John.

"Who are you?" begged the Professor grabbing John's arm.

The car door opened as John stepped out into the night air, his feet not touching any platform. The still unconscious Alexandra in his arms surrounded by the same lavender mist that still clung to the Professor. "You already know Saul. I'm John Isaac Newton, Isaac Newton's son."

chapter 3

ALEXANDRA

Alexandra opened her eyes, but was unable to raise her head. Maybe the hell she thought she had experienced was all a bad nightmare. It couldn't have happened. It just couldn't have happened. Alexandra turned her head and lifted her arms. She wanted to scream, it was no nightmare. The needle marks were all up and down her arms.

Tears started streaming down the side of her face onto the pillow and they wouldn't stop. As bad as the vision of the needle marks, the reality of her current circumstances came crashing around her. She was wearing a set of green hospital scrubs she could vaguely remember putting on. Each of her wrists had an intravenous tube attached to a small machine humming on the nightstand. She could see her blood being sucked out of one wrist by a squat whirring machine. It seemed that from the machine her blood was being pumped back into her other wrist.

Tears continued as she realized wherever she was, it was no hospital. It looked more like a cheap hotel room. She had to get away! She raised her head expecting to be nauseous, but found when she sat up she felt quite well. Her throat felt terrible, raw from all the times her stomach acid had passed up her esophagus. Other than having difficulty swallowing and the soreness in her arms, she was surprised how well she felt. She strained to see more clearly, but there was an odd purple mist clinging to her body. The more she tried to swat it away, the more it seemed to cling to her flesh. She let out a scream of frustration. It was like being covered in purple cotton candy.

The only noise, besides her one scream, was the whirring of the machine. She suddenly realized that someone was cleansing her blood. The bed she was in was clean. Her clothes had been washed, mended and folded by her bed. Her hair had been washed, but needed combed desperately. She could not even draw her fingers through her hair. There were no restraints. She could, she realized get up and leave. Get up and run, but where, where could she go? They, whoever they were, came in the middle of the night and dragged her from her dorm room. They never asked her a question. They never said who they were. They just repeatedly pumped her full of drugs. The tears started to come faster. She had to run, run, and get away.

She started by removing the needles from her veins. She found gauze on the night stand and wound it round her wrists. She didn't see any tape and was unwilling to spend any time looking for it. She kept winding the gauze around her wrists until she could no longer see any blood flow. From a night stand facing her bed she saw her reflection in a mirror. She saw how bruised and battered her body had become. They had used her as a punching bag. She told herself she looked like a cadaver she had once seen in a biology lab that had been dragged by a car.

Ignoring the reflection, she began to dress herself in the clothes she never wanted to see again. Someone had mended the rips and tears and washed away all the filth. She looked for her socks and shoes, but couldn't see them. She tried to remember if she had been wearing any shoes when they had pulled her from her dorm room. Her last memory was being dragged by her hair into a subway car. She remembered the longing for the drug, the urgency for it to be squeezed into her blood. However, she felt no need for it now. Only the overwhelming desire to run.

She went to the door expecting it to be barred, but it opened easily into a dark and somewhat shabby hall. She thought about the elevator, but noted the stairs and started her escape down the uncarpeted stairwell. As she made her way down the stairs her unshod feet partially stuck to the metal that trimmed the cement stairs. As she looked upon the wall at her first turn in the stairwell she snorted a harsh laugh at the evidence of her continued poor luck. The stairwell had the floor numbers painted on the wall and she noted she was starting down from the twenty-fifth floor. She had a long way to go and she was already beginning to become noxious. She leaned heavily on the railing trying desperately to remain upright and not fall. Maybe there was more than blood being pumped back into her body. She prayed it was not more narcotics. The windows in the stairwell were mere slits that looked like they had needed cleaned when the building was first built fifty years ago, but they had never gotten around to it. Fortunately, the windows did allow enough light to enter to allow her to navigate the stairs as most of the light bulbs needed changed. The windows also told her that it was a gray and wintery day outside.

Alexandra finally got to the last turn in the stairwell and pushed on the bar across the gray metal door covered in graffiti. She was so relieved when it opened she didn't even acknowledge the cold air. At least not for the first couple of steps, not until the cold January sleet blew into her face and her shoeless feet cracked the lite coat of ice hiding the puddle in the broken brick alley. She realized that in addition to no shoes or socks she had no coat, no identification and no money. The smell in the alley was not diminished by the cold air. If anything the chill seemed to enhance the odor, it was overpowering. The smell hit her senses and empty stomach hard and she gasped as she reminded herself, she had not yet escaped from her nightmare.

"Hey, beautiful," a voice called out from behind a dumpster. "Did'ja have a lover's spat?"

She freaked out at the sound of the deep male voice and started to run. She was running so hard and so fast the gauze she had wound around her wrists became undone and the blood rushing forth overwhelmed the gauze's ability to staunch its flow. Blood began to drip onto her palms and from there down her wrists. Her feet were fast turning blue. She could not tell if her sight was impaired because of the sleet or her tears. All she could think to do was run hard and run harder.

Alexandra ran so frantically, she was so intent on making her escape, she didn't see the bus speeding along Fifth Avenue. She ran right out in front of the hurtling vehicle. Right out in front of and into the path of her most assured death. She wrenched her head to the left just in time to see the look of shock on her unwary assassin's face, the bus driver. He didn't intend to kill her, she didn't intend to die, but it seemed to be that this was her intended fate. And then just like that, everything slowed down and the bus and Alexandra's body came to a halt, her frozen in full-stride about a foot off the ground in front of the non-moving bus. For a moment she thought this was how people die. A tiny slice of her mind, the scientific part, thought it would be a major breakthrough in the study of physics and time if she could only survive to write about it. A curtailment of time, a disconnection from reality that allowed the victim a chance to reflect on his or her life. Yet, from the corner of her eye, she saw movement. From around the corner of the bus the most beautiful boy she had ever seen was walking towards her. Walking at a languid pace. As if he had all the time in the world, while she had no time at all.

Clearly, she was about to die. Yet, here she was frozen in time, in space. She had a strange thought that this must be an angel sent to spare her the pain from the impact of the bus.

And then he spoke her name, "Alexandra," as he walked up to her and looked in her emerald eyes. It was obvious he had no concern for the fact that he too had just walked in front of the once speeding bus. "My dear Alexandra, you've so much life left to live." And with those words he scooped her up in his arms and pulled her inside his coat and moved both of them away from in front of the bus as it was released and continued to speed down Fifth Avenue. Time seemed to be brought back to its normal flow.

Enveloped in this angel's arms, she immediately became warm. Her fear evaporated the lavender haze seemed to reappear and caress her once more. However, this time she didn't try and brush it off as she somehow realized it was meant to heal her. How she knew this she had no idea. She also knew, somehow, in this man's arms, she need never be afraid. And then her exhaustion overwhelmed her and what little remaining adrenaline she had been running on evaporated, she passed out. Safe in his embrace.

It was while lying in the hotel bed from which she had just attempted to escape that an old redundant dream of hers returned with exceptional clarity. She was on a pier waiting impatiently, anxiously, hopefully with thousands of people milling about as if it was a holiday. The ship they were all waiting to leave upon was huge. Its phenomenal size nearly took up her whole view. Everyone was energized and happy around her, but Alexandra was scared, worried and very anxious. She was standing on one of the higher decks looking out over the railing. Waiting for something, waiting for someone who never appeared. Alexandra had this dream so many times in her short life. Usually it came to her in times of stress like when her foster mother passed or the night before some big exam. She had it repeatedly these past few weeks since her kidnapping. Previously, it was at this point in her dream she had always woken up. Looking out over the railing as the boat that was to somehow seal her doom slipped from its dock. Amazingly, this time as she looked to the pier the dream continued. This time her fear evaporated and her strength returned. Her anxiety disappeared. This time when she looked to the pier, she saw her angel, the same angel who had saved her from the oncoming bus, smiling broadly and waving up to her.

Alexandra's eyes flew open and she sat up in shock as she gasped for air, her heart pounding as if it was trying to escape her chest. She remembered the dream and who she thought she saw from the deck of the ship. As she looked around, she realized she was back in the hotel room from which she thought she had just recently tried to escape. She remembered the look of the bus driver as they were both held in suspension. Yet, here she was warm and dressed in the same clean and mended clothes she wore during her thwarted escape attempt. This time, however, she had on warm woolen socks. She wiggled her toes just to make sure they were all there. There was a warm glow in the room and as she gained her presence of mind, she could only stare in wonder. The odd lavender light accompanied by the soft scent of the same flower hovered over her bed and shed a soft gentle glow over her. As she sat up further it changed from lavender to lime green and emitted a soft tinkling sound, as if from the keys on the far right side of a piano. Then her angel walked in with a concerned look on his face and he sat down in the chair at the side of her bed.

"I'm sorry," he apologized. "I never should've left you alone. I didn't expect you to have the strength or the courage to get out of bed. I was afraid, if you did regain consciousness any kind of restraints would only scare you all the more." He reached behind the chair and held up a large Macy's Department Store bag, "I'd gone out to buy you some shoes and a coat. When I went to pay I realized I had no currency. It took longer than I thought."

"Who are you?" her mouth was dry and her voice cracked. He reached over and brought a glass of water to her lips. "Wait, I know you. I think, I've seen you before. Somewhere..." her voice trailed off.

"My name is John Newton. And yes, we met weeks ago in the Columbia University bookstore," he smiled.

"No," she corrected somewhat harshly. Somewhere else she thought it was on the tip of her memory when he interrupted her thoughts, her dream.

"When we touched," he paused, "When we touched it triggered the curse. You saved my life."

"I saved you, but," Alexandra looked around. "You saved me!"

He shook his head and sighed, "There's a lot I need to share with you. You've been through so much, I hardly know where to begin."

From somewhere, she never knew where, she drew on her strength, her feeling of safety here in this angel's presence. She drew on her remaining strength, smiled and simply said, "In the beginning John."

John thought he had never seen such a beautiful sight, where did she get the strength to smile he asked himself. "I'm afraid if I started in the beginning, we'd be here much longer than the time we have. It's not safe here." He noticed Alexandra shudder and continued in a calm voice, "We've some time, just not enough to tell you everything and deal with all the questions you'll have. Quite frankly, there's a lot I need to learn as well."

"For now the best explanation I can give you is my name is John Newton. We met in the basement of the Columbia University bookstore. You were after a physics book...," he said.

Alexandra cut him off and began speaking very fast, "It's you!" she exclaimed. "We touched and some sparks came out of the book and then the lights went out. When I went back for the book you were gone, but another clerk gave it to me. He said you knew I'd come back looking for it. The book was amazing every problem was solved and formulas rewritten..." Her voice trailed off as she thought she remembered who he was, where she'd seen him, the bookstore salesman sure, but somewhere else.

"Yes, that's right," John smiled. "Your touch allowed me to focus, to escape. Because of you I took that book and rewrote it. It gave me a purpose, a reason to focus, answer all the questions, correct the formulas. In doing so, it permitted me to clear my mind."

"Wow, what?" mumbled Alexandra dumbfounded as she shook her head to digest everything John had just said. None of it made any sense.

"You see Alexandra I fell in love with you when you were Princess Alexandra Friederike Auguste Von Anhalt-Zerbst Dornberg," said John.

"Uh, no," she gasped, realizing that her poor angel was demented. "You've the wrong person my name is Alexandra Holt. I'm from the foothills of West Virginia. I'm nobody." Is this what this is all about she hoped, a case of mistaken identity? Although, she felt sorry for the other Alexandra.

John responded with a look of concern, "I don't know who you think you are, but when we met for the first time we fell in love. We danced at the court of Catherine the Great, your Aunt. You are a Princess from the Anhalt family that ruled what was at the time one of the most powerful military powers on the continent, Prussia."

Alexandra, did all she could not to roll her eyes. This poor angel was sadly unhinged, she concluded.

"I lost you once before. I'm not sure how Matthew got you passed all the guards into that bookstore, but I owe you my life. And for my freedom they put you through hell to make sure I'd go back to prison to save you," said John.

Alexandra could not help herself this time she rolled her eyes. "I freed you, but you saved me! The subway... the bus!" she exclaimed.

John smiled, a brilliant smile thought Alexandra, "Look, I told you it's complicated. You'd never have been in any danger if not for freeing me, but we're losing valuable time..."

John rose from his chair and went to the window and pulled back the blind. The terrible weather had come and gone. She must have slept the night as in through the window came blindingly brilliant sunshine revealing a blue and beautiful morning.

"If you're up to it, we really should get away from here. I've used too much of the light and it leaves a trace. They're sure to track us here," said John.

"They?" she queried. "You mean those monsters. Why did they imprison you? I mean us."

He grabbed the Macy's bag removed the walking boots and began to lace them for her. "I'll tell you what. There's a coffee shop around the corner about a block from here. It has some outside tables. We'll grab a coffee. I'll try and explain things a bit better and then we'll be on our way."

She didn't really want to leave. It suddenly seemed so safe. Even so, she nodded in agreement and said, "Bathroom first."

Once again, he gave her that brilliant smile. His eyes were remarkably blue, almost like an ocean in turmoil, she thought as he nodded back.

She stood and hobbled into the bathroom. Her extra day in bed had caused every remaining muscle in her body to cramp up. She could barely stand without John's help. When she got into the bathroom and looked in the mirror, she hardly recognized herself. The whole right side of her face was deep bluish-green tinged with yellow. The bruise from where Remy had struck her only three days before. Her hair, while clean, was tangled and looked like it had not been combed in forever. She knew John wanted to flee, she could tell he was nervous, but her whole body ached. She went to the bathroom, gently washed her face, used some mouth wash and reached out to open the bathroom door to return to the bedroom. She hesitated momentarily, not certain what she would see on the other side of the door. She was surprised by the fear that suddenly engulfed her. Her hands began to shake almost uncontrollably over the door knob. She realized she didn't want to be alone, would she ever feel safe? Should John have let the bus hit her and fled himself?

She somehow managed to open the door and saw John smiling with a backpack obviously anxious to get started. He was also holding up a new winter jacket for her.

Even though she had no idea who he was, she felt her fear immediately melt away. Perhaps, she was a princess after all.

chapter 4

GOTTFRIED

The New York City weather had definitely improved. It felt more like a crisp autumn morning rather than late January. Alexandra got a few stares from the barista as her face, though significantly improved, was still off color and obviously bruised from a terrible blow. Nevertheless, since she and John were both smiling little was said. John bought several rolls as well as a cup of coffee for each of them. They had just sat down at an outside table watching all the people milling about on their way to work when suddenly there was a loud noise above and beyond the usual city cacophony. Alexandra took a while to realize it sounded like a crow. It was cawing over and over as if it was being tortured or, as was the case, providing a warning. John tensed immediately, he grabbed Alexandra's hand and started to rise. There was no look of terror on his face, but a look of determination a necessity to move immediately, as if they were late for a train.

Suddenly, out of nowhere it seemed there was a man sitting at their table. The fear she felt running down the alley instantly returned to Alexandra's body. Every muscle tensed and her teeth actually started to chatter. All activity around them froze. All the people who only moments ago had been noisily going on about their business were frozen in place. A shriek escaped from her before she even had a chance to look at John.

"Leaving so soon Johnny?" asked the apparition. He appeared to be in his early thirties. He was wearing a very expensive white suit, gray shirt with a long stylish black tie stripped in gold. He was clean shaven and wore a broad brimmed white hat as if he had just popped in from the Riviera. He exuded power and confidence. Confidence from a power that could only be supplied by evil. She knew instantly that she was face to face with the man who had ordered her kidnapping. A man who actually employed someone like Remy. This is the man who John had wanted to avoid at all cost. This had to be the man that had imprisoned them.

As John scanned the scene around him, he portrayed neither fear nor concern. The fact that everything around them was suspended in animation seemed to not surprise him in the least. He looked at Alexandra nodded to her and sat down. As they reclaimed their seats a series of huge men began to appear all around them. They were not frozen and they all faced John and Alexandra until the couple was completely hemmed in by over fifty brutish looking men. All of them wore suits and many had on reflective sunglasses. The men were of various ethnicities while more than a few were terribly scarred and disfigured. There were no women.

It was an army. My God thought Alexandra, what is going on? We're so done for. Despite John's look of nonchalance she could not stop the flow of tears that had begun to run down her battered face.

"Herr Leibniz, how nice to see you after all these years," John paused. "Well, actually to tell you the truth, Gottfried, I must say it's not actually nice at all." Looking around at all the men John continued, "My, my you do have a lot of mouths to feed. You've had time to train all these men?" His tone was one of running into a past acquaintance that one really didn't want to meet. He was unsmiling and seemed to be taking time to observe everything. Alexandra on the other hand could not help continuing to cry and start to shake as if suddenly the temperature had fallen to subzero. She gave out another little shriek with the appearance of Remy.

"Time has been kind to me Johnny. I'm sure you can appreciate how much can be accomplished when there is no interference from meddlers," said Gottfried in a very heavy German accent.

He nodded to the girl by John's side who was now on the verge of hysteria, "But Johnny how rude of you. You neglected to introduce me to your," Gottfried looked at Alexandra, who by this time was a complete wreck, "Well, I was about to say freudin (*girlfriend*), but Johnny I think you can do better." He said this loud enough to be heard by all his men and none laughed louder than Remy.

When John did not respond to the taunt or make any attempt to introduce her, Gottfried waved a hand and continued, "Matthew was very clever. I give him all the credit for getting you this far Johnny but your time has passed. You either go back or we finish it here."

As he said this there was a loud cawing once again echoing down through the canyon of the city buildings. The bird seemed to defy the paralysis placed on the rest of the city. Gottfried turned to one of his minions," Jacob, you and Otto go get that damn crow. Two huge men peeled out of the back row and started to fly, physically fly, toward the sound of the cawing.

As they left Gottfried added, "Be careful, Matthew must be nearby!"

"Raven," John corrected with a whisper.

"Was (*What*)?" asked Gottfried perturbed by the correction.

"It's a raven, not a crow and I'm sorry for your loss of Otto and Jacob. Were they with you long?" asked John even softer.

"Well, that's right! You used to have a flea bitten crow following you about. So, not just any crow," replied Gottfried ignoring the fact that it was a raven and not a crow. He added, "Max, go assist them!"

"So, where were we?" Gottfried gave a nod toward Alexandra as if to thank her for stopping the shedding of more tears. "Yes, without your meddling Johnny, things have been going quite well. Quite well indeed."

"Bedlam," interrupted John.

"Well, some might see chaos Johnny. However, it's from conflict that strength rises and Auftrag (*order*) ultimately prevails," smiled Gottfried as if expounding on a course in ethics.

"Does strength, as you define it, require the beating and drugging of defenseless women?" John looked around at all the bodies, all the might arrayed against him. For the first time he raised his voice so all of them could hear him. "Gottfried has never been able to control the power he's introduced to you. If you continue to follow him you'll all perish terribly. Look at Remy. Walk away now before it's too late! This will be the only warning I give you."

Alexandra looked at him as if he were mad! In the mountains of West Virginia, where Alexandra grew up, you learned early in life not to prod a rattle snake.

Gottfried took the bait and yelled in a mocking tone, "Ah, semantics after forty years we come back to the old debates. Newton the virtuous. Newton the holy. Newton the only one capable of divining God's purpose. You and Matthew brought the girl into play. You always blame me for your indiscretions!" Gottfried suddenly pounded his fist on the table which held its place only momentarily before shattering into pieces. John had somehow seen this coming and he had grabbed his coffee before the table collapsed. Alexandra's coffee was not so fortunate and it fell to the ground, spreading out over the cement.

Alexandra in surprise let out yet a third shriek.

Once again, there was a loud caw and Gottfried yelled, "Can no one deal with that damn krähe (*crow*)? Jenner, take two men and get rid of it!"

"Gottfried, do you think that's wise?" asked Jenner. He regretted it as soon as the words left his mouth.

Gottfried never looked back at the man called Jenner. Instead he gave a simple glance toward Remy, the monster from the train currently wearing a patch over one eye. Remy stepped forward and with a slash of his wrist caused Jenner's throat to explode in a fountain of blood. He then turned to Alexandra, grinned, winked with his unpatched eye and said, "Hello beautiful, remember me?" His grin was short lived as an invisible force seemed to cause his body to jerk while his spine and foot twisted further inward. He fell to his hands and knees before straightening back up and grinning at Alexandra.

Alexandra screamed again as along with the recognition of Remy, her face and hair had been sprayed with Jenner's blood. She was so shocked she started to rise to run, but John, who had also been spattered instantly grabbed her arm and pulled her back into her chair. Gottfried's white suit was unblemished. Remy had controlled the flow of his victim's blood so as not to blemish his master's suit, but indeed spill out over John and in particular Alexandra.

The crow gave out another yell! Gottfried screamed, "It's a goddamn black krähe (*crow*) someone get rid of it!" Two men from the back row ran down the street. John knew neither would be looking for the Raven, but they undoubtedly would meet up regardless.

The body count facing John had been reduced by six, down about twelve percent from just minutes ago. Everything had gone exceptionally well, but he knew time was running out. "I guess having so many to train means few get the attention they need, eh Gottfried?" asked John dismissively.

Alexandria was by his side shaking, her teeth chattering, uncontrollably begging John inwardly to stop provoking this insane megalomaniac.

Gottfried regained his composure, "Maybe I should get a murder of crows?" he mused. "But enough of this Johnny. It's back to the tomb for you, and the girl? Well, well…" He paused as if seeing her for the first time, "Remy was right. She's as pretty as the first one I had killed." He grinned and began to laugh evilly as he reached out and clutched Alexandra's chin in his ice cold fingers.

At Gottfried's icy touch, Alexandra's fear all but exploded within her. She pulled away from the touch instinctively and rose to run despite John's hand on her arm attempting to hold her in place. As she pushed back her chair, a man who had been crowding her since his appearance suddenly fell to the ground. He fell silently at her feet, no blood, and no muscle movements of any kind. There had been no warning. John hadn't even looked at him. Simultaneously a second man, the one immediately to John's right crumpled to the ground. It was happening so quickly. It had caught Gottfried off guard, he turned and saw two more of his troops crumble to the pavement.

"Nein!" Gottfried yelled at John. "Unmoglich Sie nicht so stark sein kann. (*It's impossible, you can't be that strong!*)"

"Alle müssen Sie jetzt konzentrieren (*All of you need to focus now!*)" Gottfried screamed at the top of his voice. The remaining forty or so of Gottfried's men all began staring at John as if they could will him back into a state of captivity. It was as if they were all calling on some unseen power. It was in fact how Gottfried had done it the last time. John had been isolated and exhausted, having used all his energy saving a dying man. In that weakened state Gottfried had only needed six lieutenants to subdue him. He had well over six times that number with him now.

This time, however, John was at near full strength and he was well aware of the meaning and nature of Gottfried's last taunt. Despite the opposing group's combined invisible strength more of Gottfried's henchmen began to fall. Two more near John fell both men bleeding from their ears, mouth and nostrils. John had been able to discern those among Gottfried's men, which were living with to date undetected illnesses. He was able to cause heart failure in some and in others to speed up strokes or aneurysms. Finally, John noticed two with epilepsy. When these men had their disease triggered by John they fell to the pavement foaming at the mouth and twitching uncontrollably. This appeared to unnerve Gottfried's men even more than those having fallen from no apparent cause.

Gottfried was sweating, straining as he focused on John. The veins on his brow and neck started to bulge. Alexandra noticed a foul smell and a thick smoke start to form around her feet. It was at this point two things happened within seconds of each other. First one of Gottfried's strongest lieutenants fell into him, causing Gottfried to momentarily lose concentration. And then, a raven, as if waiting for this to happen, flew down into the battle and pecked and scratched at Gottfried's face despite the wide brim of his white hat. With a scream of rage Gottfried lashed out at the bird and in so doing completely lost his concentration. As Gottfried faltered so did his army of henchmen as all eyes were on the bird and its vicious unrelenting attack.

Alexandra, who just moments before had stood up to run became transfixed, like everyone else at the café, by the ferocity of the bird's attack. The last thing Alexandra saw was blood spraying from Gottfried's face where the valiant raven was clawing at the German's eyes. Blood was spurting onto Gottfried's once clean white suit. It was at that instant that John grabbed her wrist and they disappeared with a crack into blueish light and vapor.

Her first thought was that she was about to die. The scream she let out this time was her best yet and it did not stop. She was so afraid and she was shaking so violently that without John's strength she would have been unable to retain her sanity. Once John had grabbed her wrist it was as if the two of them had jumped off the viewing platform at Niagara Falls. There was a roar of sound like a waterfall, but there was no moisture.

They seemed to be picking up speed and as she was about to scream again two things happened, first, her curiosity overcame her fear as she noticed people and images falling by the wayside. At this point she somehow correctly gathered that they were falling through time. The second thing that came about was she heard John's voice in her mind. Not her ear because it would not have been able to overcome the roar or rush of events speeding by. In her mind, she heard John's voice, "Leave your fear behind and trust in the Lord."

His words somehow immediately calmed her jumbled nerves. She didn't understand exactly what he meant, but it was as if he had shared some of his power with her. She tapped into this strength, into his power and she was no longer scared. Suddenly she remembered her epiphany while being carried away from the bus in his arms, as long as she stayed near this man she need never be afraid again.

chapter 5

THE DANCE

Alexandra was looking at her clothes and hair once again splattered with foul blood, blood from a dying man. When she woke up only moments ago, she had been face down on a beach with the surf breaking behind her. It was very warm and a beautiful scented breeze was blowing through the palm trees. The contrast with New York City and its winter morning could not have been greater. She looked over at John who had not yet gained consciousness. She was winded, but otherwise in good shape. She didn't have much to go upon but given the dryness and coloring of the blood on her clothing, she realized she must have been unconscious herself for some time. The rest had done her good. The trauma of having met Gottfried and seeing Remy again seemed to have been partially offset by the amazement of the trip. The journey from the café to the beach had not been short. She had seen so many images and faces pass by she felt certain they must have traversed a significant period of time.

As she sat up, she was struck by a wave of nausea and it forced her to lay back down. She tried gazing up into the sky and focus on the cloud formations. After a few minutes when the world finally seemed to stop spinning, she thought she heard water trickling nearby. She crawled over to a small pond and splashed her face and cupped her hands to drink some water. She thought nothing had ever tasted so refreshing. She tore off a sleeve of her battered blouse and dipped it in the pool. She took it over to apply to John's forehead. John seemed to be breathing and his pulse seemed strong. She could only hope he was resting. Perhaps the heat of the battle and the trip had exhausted him. Otherwise, she thought to herself this is going to be one short prison break.

The aqua surf continued to roll in over a pure white beach. The area they had landed in appeared completely deserted with not even a bird in the air. Not even the poor raven that had saved their lives. She gave another unwilling shudder at the thought of what they had just escaped from and tried to make sense of all that had happened. How did that bird know when to strike? It was as if John and the raven had coordinated the whole event. How was it that John was able to kill all those men in seconds? Who was Gottfried and that evil troll of a man, Remy? And what, my God, whatever did they want from her? As time went by, and John continued to rest, Alexandra tried to make sense in her own mind all of the events that had brought her to this deserted beach. At least, the monotonous sound of the surf breaking and the touch of the gentle breeze seemed to calm her nerves. Finally, after admitting she was at a loss to explain anything that had happened, she just sat down next to John and waited for him to explain where they were.

Finally, John began to stir a bit, but he still didn't open his eyes. She had already made an attempt to wash his face and hands to remove all of Jenner's and Gottfried's dried blood. She had also tried to position his head using the coat John had bought her to give his neck some support. Alexandra looked around and thought about calling for help but it was so desolate and the surf though relatively calm would have drowned out any yell. She was so shattered by recent events she had to fight off the urge to leave John and run away. Then once again, she remembered the feeling she had when all seemed lost and that being by his side made her feel safe. Instead of running away, she stroked John's hair and kept him in the shade of her body.

As the sound of the surf gently drifted away and the sun began to set, she leaned over further and kissed him. She wasn't sure who or even what he was, but somehow she knew he would protect her with all his strength. It was with that kiss that John finally opened his eyes.

He smiled weakly as their eyes, emerald and the sapphire, met. His head was in her lap. He closed his eyes and left out a long sigh of exhaustion, "It's been so long, so very long. I can't remember the last time I could close my eyes and sleep. They never allowed me to sleep. They thought I'd escape them in my dreams. How long it's been since I've felt safe."

"Are we safe John?" Alexandra prayed it was so, "Do you even know where we are?"

John sat up slowly and as he looked around a beautiful smile spread across his face. "We're on an island in the Bahamas, Exuma. The year is 1715. And no, we'll never be entirely safe until Gottfried is either dead or repentant. Which for all practical purposes means dead. However, we are about as safe as we can be at this stage."

Alexandra just stared at him in disbelief. "How?" was all she could get out.

John rubbed her cheek to remove some dried blood, "You've been through hell. I just woke up from hell. To say you deserve an explanation is an understatement."

He rose to his feet, swayed a bit and extended his hand to help her up. "I owe you an explanation, but they say a picture is worth, a thousand words. Come, walk with me a bit. It'll do us both some good."

Alexandra took John's hand and allowed herself to be pulled to her feet. The weather was near perfect as they walked along the beach and though the sun once high in the sky had begun to descend it was still warm. They walked hand in hand after having removed their shoes and socks which they stuffed into John's backpack. After a few hundred yards John pulled from his backpack the rolls they had purchased that very morning at the café. Alexandra, famished, thought she had never tasted anything so good. They walked along the water's edge so that their feet could greet the warm salt water as it came ashore. They had walked about a mile when Alexandra left out a yell, "look a ship!"

"It's the *Principia*," responded John. "I'd hoped to find her here". The *Principia* was a small two-masted sloop. It wasn't a modern vessel. Indeed, it looked to have been made in the eighteenth century. The masts and spars were tattered and torn. The sails were shredded but the hull appeared to be in one piece. The worst that could be said about her was that she sat beached in about six feet of sand.

"Matthew, the Raven and I were here on a mission when we were overtaken by a hurricane. Our crew took the opportunity to swim for shore while Matthew and I salvaged the ship. We were able to beach her here. The next day after we took a break to recover we were overcome by the beauty of this place. We decided then if we ever got split up, this is the place and the time we would meet."

"It's beautiful here," agreed Alexandra, although somewhat underwhelmed by the condition of the boat. She had no idea who Matthew was that John referred to, but she remembered Gottfried had also mentioned the name. She gathered the Raven was the bird that had helped them escape. Putting all this aside she asked, "But, can you explain how we got here! We were about to be killed by about fifty men in New York City. How did we get here to this period in time?" There wasn't panic in her voice but it was steely. She wanted some answers.

"Alexandra," said John, "You've only seen the dark side of my world. I need to show you the beauty." With that John, grabbed Alexandra's hand and casually lifted his chin. Alexandra caught a flash of yellow light out of the corner of her eye. They rose, flew, the remaining hundred yards up and onto the deck of the wreck, the *Principia*.

Alexandra let out a screech and flung her arms around John's neck as they gently floated onto the ship's deck. "How?" her eyes were wide, not in shock or fear, but awe.

"This ship was a bit ahead of her time. Down in the captain's cabin, the first door you see on the right as you go down the stairs, is a shower. I'll make sure the water is hot. While you're in the shower, I'll find you some clean clothes, something with a little less blood." They both smiled at that comment. "Take your time. When you come up I'll present you with a picture of my world," said John.

John held open the door for her, but Alexandra hesitated as she looked down into the hold it was pitch black. "It's safe," John reassured her. He clicked his fingers and a soft lime-green ball of light, about the size and weight of a tennis ball, appeared in his hand. He handed it to her and clicking his fingers again, it somehow emitted a gentle pulse which added a sense of security in addition to its light.

"How?" she looked at the ball in wonder.

"Squeeze it harder and the light will grow brighter," added John with a bemused look.

As Alexandra, squeezed the lime green tennis-ball-like object the light indeed became more intense. She smiled, holding the ball and slowly stepped down into the deck below. It was a small ship, but she could tell it was of the highest craftsmanship. While the sails had been tattered and the ship appeared as though it had been abandoned after a fierce storm, the hold of the ship was dry and immaculate. The woodwork was absolutely fantastic.

After entering what she took to be the captain's cabin she placed the green globe on the edge of a desk and looked around. It was indeed as if she awoke back in time, even down to the kerosene lantern which she did not need. A log book was open and she glimpsed the date, July 31, 1715. There was no plastic, no computer screens nothing from the time they had abandoned. Everything that surrounded her was made of polished wood and brass, pewter and iron fixtures.

If not for the needle marks on her arms, she would have thought this all a nightmare. A bad trip... but then until she was kidnapped, she'd never used drugs. So the reality of the needle marks on her arm could only be real if the kidnapping had occurred. This was not a dream, but her life gone inexplicably askew. She gently pressed her fingers over the maps laid out over a huge desk, a quill and brass compass. "What is this place?" she murmured to herself. "What have you got yourself into Alexandra?"

She saw the side room John had referred to and she entered to see a shower, towels and even soap. "When was the last time I washed," she asked herself. She shrugged off her ill-used clothes and stepped into a small wooden cylinder of a room and pulled a chain. She was immediately drenched in warm water. Water that grew warmer the longer she pulled down on the chain. Heaven could not be sweeter than this she thought.

Alexandra, who originally was in a hurry to get back to John and learn what this was all about could not seem to be able to gain the necessary energy to leave the warm, now scalding, shower. Tears almost came, perhaps they did and the hot water washed them away. In any case, it was close to a half-hour before she could pry herself out of the shower.

She spent a long time in the little cabin outside the shower, drying off her body with the largest cotton towel she had ever seen. The mirror she discovered, revealed a not so pretty picture. She was emaciated. She hadn't had a good meal in forever. In fact, other than the rolls from the café John provided her on the walk to this ship, she could not remember keeping much of any other food down since her kidnapping. The good news was that the right side of her face that had been so deeply bruised, had miraculously healed. She looked down at her arms expecting to see the needle marks, but was thrilled when she found they too had vanished. If only that shower could wash away the memories she thought. As she looked at her hair, she almost started crying again what a disaster. She grabbed the green orb trying to get a better picture of what she had to deal with when the ball started to emit a soft lavender light. She swept it near her hair and the light swept away all of the knots and left a mane of blonde hair she never realized she owned. It wasn't even blonde anymore, it was golden.

She walked away from the mirror, feeling remarkably better but the thought of pulling her blood splattered clothes on again repulsed her. Wrapped in the towel she stepped out to look for something to wear when she found her ragged and bloodstained clothes had been replaced with a dazzling white gown along with a diamond encrusted tiara. There was a string of pearls with a set earrings to match of the highest beauty. Beside the dress was a set of diamond encrusted ballet slippers that she knew would fit perfectly. As if this was not enough from the outside of the vessel, drifting down to where she was in the captain's cabin, she couldn't believe her ears. There was a piano playing and whoever was playing was incredible (5A). She had to have gone insane, she thought. She was living in a dream world. It was the only possible explanation.

[Music "The Heart Asks Pleasure First" by Myleene Klass] https://www.youtube.com/watch?v=iGJmON1fr-g

Alexandra Holt from West Virginia had gone down into the hold of a broken ship a castaway she came out a princess, but not just any princess, Princess Alexandra Friederike Auguste Von Anholt-Zerbst Dornburg. The Prussian Princess who captured the breath of Catherine the Great's Russian court and dazzled one and all with her beauty and charm. The Princess whose dance card contained the names of a hundred hopeful suitors.

The song that came from the shore floated in and out of Alexandra's hearing as the surf beat on the seashore. As she looked for a means to descend from the ship a staircase magically materialized and gave her access to the beach. Alexandra took her first step onto the beach and realized her ballet slippers were not made for the sand. She brought her shoes up one at a time and removed them as she stepped on the sand in her bare feet. With the train of her dress following her in the sand, she walked toward the sound of the piano and found John playing beautifully on a magnificent grand piano with what she realized was probably the first waltz-like music she had ever heard. Growing up in West Virginia she had grown up on a bit more edgy music.

John stopped at once when he saw her and said, "my lady!" He rose and gave a slight bow and crossed over to greet her. He gently took her hand and kissed the back of it. John had managed to clean up as well and was dressed in an elegant white uniform of the highest quality.

Alexandria blushed holding up her sandals, "I suspect," she stated. "Although I have no proof, but I suspect that few princesses walk on sandy beaches without shoes while their gown is dragged through the sand."

John bemused said, "You must wear your dancing shoes my lady, to dance our waltz."

Alexandra, playfully suggested in mock horror, "And how is one to dance a waltz in the sand? And John, while the music was nice the clothes are amazing. You're awesome, but you promised me some sort of explanation. You said I saved you. None of what I went through, I'm certain, had anything to do with me. I'm pretty confident right now this is all a case of mistaken identity. John I need some clarity!" she had started out stating this in a calm, steady voice, but by the end it was in a rising tone and approaching hysteria.

"Now!" she cried out as she felt tears welling up inside of her.

John merely knelt before her and removing her slippers from her hand slipped them back on her feet. He rose smiled and snapped his fingers. Behind him a whole orchestra appeared and started to play the song she had first heard in the captain's cabin. This time, however, it was not just a piano, but a full orchestra, including violins and cellos. "I've gone totally insane," she murmured.

Alexandra could not make out their faces, but there must have been forty or fifty musicians. The music they started out to play was unknown to her, but it touched her soul. "How does one dance on wet sand?" she finally smiled, having given up the hope she was going to hear any sort of an explanation.

"Oh, we can't dance on the sand, my lady, our dance floor is the sea," and with that said John led her away from the orchestra out onto the now calm sea. The surf which until now had never been still, sat as quiet as a pond with no breeze. Alexandra's first step onto the quieted sea was like a step onto a frozen pool. They began by dancing on a floor provided by the still water. As the music of the full orchestra reached a crescendo Alexandra found herself holding tightly to John as he led them above the water and they glided up into the air. The moon had risen and their dance was outlined by the light of a full moon with a million stars glittering on the edges of its light.

Alexandra, at one point that day, had felt like the life had been sucked out of her body. This dance, moving higher and higher linked in John's arms with the music pumping in her ears into her veins, gave her back her life. As the music stopped, they gently floated down through the moonlight onto the sandy beach. The surf returned to its gentle motion. She could not control her breathing, her thoughts, "How?" was the only word she could get to escape from her lips.

Her gaze was focused on John and only John. He had been transformed into a prince complete with a saber by his side. "Kind of takes your breath away," suggested John.

Alexandra gulped for air. The exhilaration of the dance, the music had indeed taken her breath away. "Who are you?" She whispered into his ear as the moon light sparkled on her tiara, her eyes, and her gold hair. "What are you? Am I even here?" asked Alexandra.

"My name is John Isaac Newton, Isaac Newton's only son. My father was a remarkable man. He unearthed many secrets in his time and he shared many, if not all of them, with me. He taught me how to live with God, for God and how to be one with his Holy Spirit."

Alexandra looked at him with complete incredulity. She would not have believed a word if not for the inconceivable dance they had just shared. "Isaac Newton, the Isaac Newton, who discovered the formula for gravity and invented calculus? But that Isaac Newton was born in the 1600's?" she squeaked breathlessly shaking her head. She tried to remember what little she knew of the great scientist, but her brain seemed to refuse to work. "He died in 1720 something," she said.

"All true, except he never died," said John.

"Again," said Alexandra firmly.

"He never died," said John.

She couldn't comprehend anything John was telling her. She couldn't think anymore. So she simply asked with a demure smile, "May we dance again?"

[Music "Italian Summer" by Brian Crain] https://www.youtube.com/watch?v=DHfgLZFeJTE

And with a click of his fingers the orchestra reappeared *(5B)*. He turned to face the beautiful Prussian Princess and once again they twirled and moved into the air leaving an aquamarine mist on the water as a wan yellow light accompanied them into the light provided by the full moon. The rhythm of the song seemed to encourage the surf below to reignite and somehow it miraculously kept in sync with the music. As they reached the height of their distance from the ground as the new and intoxicating music reached a crescendo, Alexandra smiled and whispered in John's ear, "I believe anything you would have me believe."

chapter 6

MATTHEW

As they floated back to earth the music stopped and the symphony dissolved. Just as Alexandra was at the point of anticipating a kiss from John the romantic air of the evening was suddenly interrupted by the sound of loud clapping of a lone man in a kilt. He was standing on the beach by the *Principia* looking over at Alexandra and John. Alexandra was about to scream, but fortunately she looked at John first who was smiling broadly.

"Thought ye'd begin the celebration without me?" yelled the man with a thick Scottish accent from the beach.

"Well," responded John, "Alexandra was demanding answers and I was afraid you'd be bringing along those dreadful bagpipes."

"Dreadful indeed!" shouted the figure from the beach and he started to play bagpipes that seemed to materialize out of thin air. The sound from the single instrument compared poorly to the music from the entire orchestra. John looked at Alexandra and mouthed, "Sorry!" as if to apologize for the racket.

Even so, as she was about to answer with a grimace and a smile, the man on the beach spread out his right arm and a hundred or more bagpipe players appeared at his side. Alexandra mouthed, "Incredible".

John did not hide his grimace at Alexandra's comment. For despite the exuberance displayed by the bagpipers before Alexandra's compliment, the compliment had barely escaped Alexandra's lips when the number of bagpipers seemed to double. Soon the number in the group was enhanced with another hundred kilted Scotsmen playing drums.

As the music came to an end, John and Alexandra floated over to what had appeared from afar to be a regimental band only to find the solitary figure when they came by his side. Once they arrived, the music stopped and the bagpipes disappeared. The Scot, what else could he be with a red beard and long red hair, tears of joy flowing down his face gave out a mighty roar. John seemed to be a solid, well fit man. The Scot was a huge bear of a man. The two men embraced each other and both were weeping tears of joy. And then the mysterious raven flew to John's shoulder and hopped up and down cawing loudly as it did so. Alexandra thought she had never seen three beings so happy, so happy to be together! Their happiness was contagious and she felt its warm embrace.

Alexandra had stood a few steps from John's shoulder as these three were so obviously overjoyed to be reunited. The two men proceeded to thump each other on the back laughing while the raven emitted a piercing caw the whole time now circling above them. Suddenly, the Scot reached over and pulled Alexandra into a bear hug that easily encompassed both her and John. The hug was from a man that tended to forget the extent of his massive strength. He all but crushed Alexandra's ribs. The hug had also left her ballet slippers behind in the sand. Meanwhile, the Raven continued to fly around them in a circle cawing exuberantly.

Finally, John broke away and said, "First things first, Alexandra, this magnificent specimen of Scottish ancestry, whom you may have already met, is my very best friend Matthew Ezekiel Scott. Other than his poor taste in music he is incredibly talented."

Alexandra standing in an eighteenth century gown with a tiara in her golden hair seemed to automatically act the part and curtsied to Matthew.

Matthew seemed taken aback for a moment, smiled and bowed at the waist, "My lady, tis an honor, but I've known ye all your young life."

Alexandra was startled at the comment. She looked at John and then at Matthew and said, "Matthew, that isn't possible. I'm sure I would have remembered meeting you."

"Aye, and I'll explain," said Matthew.

Alexandra added quickly under her breath, "I would enjoy hearing at least one explanation."

"Let me begin by say'n I'm so sorry lassie," the Scot said while trying to catch his breath and dry the tears of joy in the corner of his eyes, "I'd no idea they'd do to ya what they done. I ne'er thought Gottfried capable of such vile filth."

"You knew?" asked John taken aback by the Scot's confession. John looked upset that the man may have been willing to sacrifice Alexandra.

"Aye, but I could na see any way to get to her. When you and Alexandra touched and locked eyes it set off the colors in a way the Raven and I never imagined. Of course, we hoped it would bridge the curse and you'd pick up that terribly written physics book and correct it. We hoped it would get ya to focus and break the spell that was all part of the plan. What happened between the two of ya, however, never entered our wildest imagination. When you two touched, the colors just blew out of the book which set off all their alarms. They over reacted and flooded the bookstore with the shadows the concentration of which was beyond anything I'd ever seen. Then they kidnapped Alexandra a couple of days later when they discovered what had set off their alarms. There were so many of them John. Once the sparks came out in the bookstore, they tripled the security around you. You had awoken and I couldn't even get to ya to help ya. I tried to use that professor. I used the Way to lead him to where they were holding Alexandra and encouraged him to go to the police. They intercepted him on the steps to the station and beat him something fierce. I think they meant to kill him, but I used the Way to put him back together. Then I lost the Professor and you disappeared and I had no idea where you'd gone. My only hope was that once you escaped, together we could free Alexandra. If I tried to rescue Alexandra and failed, well, all hope of rescuing you would have been jeopardized. You see, John, I'm all that's left in the present," said Matthew sadly.

Alexandra listened to everything Matthew said not understanding what any of it meant. Her silence reflected the fact she was waiting for an opportunity to ask a question and get some clarity. John, however, was stunned by the Scot's news. "Everyone?" he asked weakly.

"Except for the Raven here," said Matthew as the Raven gave out a soft caw. "And he doesn't communicate with me like he does with you John. Together, we've been trying to get you out of New York City for the last forty years."

John, his legs buckling, fell down to the beach on his knees, "Hooke, Halley, Cotes, Whiston and Wren," asked John in dismay and horror.

"They all slipped into the future John. They'll be look' n for Isaac," whispered Matthew softly.

"You lost friends?" asked Alexandra. She wanted to pepper Matthew with questions, but she could see how hard the blow of the loss of his friends affected John.

John nodded as if unable to take in the loss. "I should've realized. There was so many of them at the coffee shop to see us off. He never could have gained so much power unless he was completely unfettered," said John.

"Unfettered is a nice way of putting it. But how, how in the world did you two ever escape! How did ye do it John?" implored the Scot squatting down to stare into John's eyes. The raven wanting to hear the answer as well flew over to sit on Matthew's shoulder.

John got a far off look in his eyes, perhaps unwilling or simply unable to accept the loss of his friends. He shook his head as if trying to clear his mind and put the mourning of his friends off for another moment. He then attempted to describe from his perspective what took place at the café, "It was amazing Matthew. When Gottfried froze the present, the Way came to me in such a dazzling array. I didn't even call for it, it came to me and offered help! The colors were never more vivid. It was as if they had been waiting for me to call on them for forty years. There was such power offered up to me the shadows couldn't have overwhelmed the light in a million years. The more Gottfried and his band tried to bring up the dark embers the more the light strengthened. Unlike from what you described that took place in the bookstore, the shadows never even floated above the pavement. I could see everyone's weaknesses, well, except for Gottfried and Remy."

At the mention of Remy's name Alexandra shuddered and Matthew spit in the sand and said "I'd ave liked very much for ye to have brought that monster to his end."

"Yes, I tried obviously for the both of them, but the shadows hid their favorites. I was able, by using a gray light to enhance many of their weaknesses and illnesses and at least collapse or shrink almost all of their powers," explained John. "I thought I might be able to end it once and for all but somehow the Raven knew it was time to leave. When he attacked Gottfried it made me realize my sight and indeed my strength was faltering. If I'd waited a second longer I doubt I would've had the strength to get Alexandra here. As it was, we had quite a hard ride." He finished with a sigh and the Raven let out a caw of acknowledgement.

"My word, John I swear I ne'er seen a man alive do what you did!" whispered Matthew.

"The men Gottfried sent after you and the Raven what happened to them?" asked John.

"Fortunately," replied Matthew, "Gottfried sent them in pairs and a few at a time. I got them to hack away at each other. We got three of them. The last pair just kept running so we let'm go."

John nodded and closing his eyes pulled out of thin air a three dimensional hologram of the New York City café from which they had just escaped. Seated around the table were Gottfried, John and Alexandra. The rest of the original fifty odd figures were displayed in such a fashion that John could see the features of each. He was able to manipulate the hologram and with Matthew's help they were able to identify each and every member at the café. From the inspection it could be seen that many of the men were scared and several severely disfigured.

"There's so many of them John," said Matthew, "We'll have to split them up."

"If he's foolish enough to permit us." said John. "Still, we were able to take out fifteen in one encounter. Alexandra and I took out three more on a subway car three days ago. If they thought themselves invulnerable, well, they no longer do."

Matthew sighed "Well, we escaped, but we're still on the run." He snapped his fingers and the schooner with tattered sails seemingly run aground in six-foot of sand became animated. A red light appeared to encircle the ship and in a ghostly hue the sloop seemed to repair itself. There was a little pop and the whole ship looked better than new. Another click, and the ship pushed itself from the sand and then began to inch itself toward the four former castaways despite the fact there was no breeze.

Matthew nodded at John and Alexandra, "I feel a wee bit unprotected on this beach. I'll feel a might better adrift at sea."

Alexandra, had been quietly taking in the joyous reunion and the sketchy details of their successful escape, but she had just about enough, "I still haven't had any explanation as to what the hell this is all about. The music, the dance," she nodded at the beach, "was amazing, but who the hell are you guys! Why was I kidnapped and pumped full of drugs. Please tell me something I can comprehend!"

Matthew looked shocked, "Ya mean to say John ya haven't explained anything to the lassie?"

John smiled, "Well to put it bluntly, we been a wee bit busy trying to stay alive." He extended his hand to Alexandra who needed both of her hands to pull John up. Then, as he magically guided her up onto the ship her clothes transformed from a flowing gown, sand filled ballet slippers and tiara to rolled-up jeans, a windbreaker and fashionable boat shoes.

"How?" asked Alexandra yet again observing a trace of both a red and a canary yellow mist that had surrounded her as she landed on the deck.

"When I have something to work with I can mend or transform clothing or shoes. Back at the hotel you had no shoes so I had to go and buy you a pair," said John misinterpreting the question.

"Oh, I swear you're going to drive me insane!" exclaimed Alexandra laughing.

John offered, "You of all people deserve an explanation. Let's get underway, then I'll explain who we are and then," he said, turning to Matthew, "we'll learn who you are."

Once they were all aboard the new sails of the now pristine craft picked up a materialized gust of wind and they gracefully drifted out to sea. Since there seemed to be no need of a crew, the three of them sat in deck chairs that also seemed to appear out of thin air and the ship lazily drifted into the magical beauty of the now rising sun. If it wasn't planned thought Alexandra, it was the most beautiful coincidence in the world.

"As I did tell you my father is Isaac Newton. You're studying Physics what do you know about him?" asked John as they lazily drifted away from the Bahamas.

"Actually, I've come across him quite a bit in my studies. He was such an amazing man," began Alexandra.

"Is an amazing man. He's still alive," interrupted Matthew.

Alexandra rolled her eyes, "Well, you asked me what I know about him and to me, well, he lived in the 1600's so to me he'd be dead. He discovered and developed the formula for gravity and was credited with the conception of calculus. He was able to calculate the mass of the planets and accurately calculate their paths. He was a great theologian and I think attempted alchemy. I read he lived an unusually long life for the early eighteenth century, into his late eighties. But as I recall, he never married."

"Not bad, but not completely accurate," said John. "I'm glad you at least have heard of him so this will make the explanation a little easier to accept. Where to begin?" he paused. "I guess it all began with the great plague of 1666. My father was in his early twenties at that time and when the plague hit London, he left Cambridge University, where he was studying, and went back to his mother's and step-father's farm. He came down with an illness that they thought at first might be the plague, but it wasn't, thank goodness. But it was very serious and they feared for his life. He was nursed back to health by a beautiful woman named Marie Oser, whom he quietly married against my grandmother's wishes. She was catholic and my father's career would have been over before it got started. So they married in secrecy and after a year they had me. Unfortunately, my father was handed a tragic and difficult decision at my birth. The doctor told my father that it was a breech birth and he was given the choice of saving me or my mother whom he dearly loved. Back then so few children grew into adulthood, it was a common choice to save the life of the mother. My father told me once, the only time he talked about it to me, that he had received a vision as he prayed for guidance that said he was to protect his son at all costs. As such, he chose me over his young wife. He would never remarry. Let me be clear, my father devoted himself to me and I never lacked for love despite all the love he gave up for me."

"My father stayed for several years until after the plague had died down and the city, London, recovered from the fire of 1667 which had destroyed half of London. Between the two catastrophes almost a quarter of London's population had been lost in two short years. In my youth, father worked as a Professor at Cambridge University and later as a Member of Parliament. He made frequent trips from London back to Woolsthorpe, the manor he eventually inherited. Early in his studies, he spent most of his time studying and searching for the philosopher's stone," said John.

When Alexandra rolled her eyes yet again Matthew chimed in, "He found it lassie that and so much more."

"Indeed, much more," added John.

Alexandra looked shocked, "But John, the philosopher's stone is the... I mean it's supposed to allow eternal life? Surely, you're not saying?"

"We're living proof lassie," said Matthew.

"My father, discovered the philosopher's stone and as Matthew suggests we are the proof. Where was I, yes, well after writing *'The Philosophiae Naturals Principia Mathmatica'*, it took us two years to write, his future was assured. As you know it provided the three laws of motion and the theory of universal gravitation."

"Us?" Interrupted Alex with a smile.

"Well, I," John blushed a bit. "I did a lot of the math. I was in my early twenties at the time."

Matthew chuckled, "The apple did not fall far from the tree."

"Anyhow, shortly after the pamphlet was published he was elected to Parliament and then subsequently he was named Master of the Mint. A position he held for the remainder of his time with us," said John.

"And why not," said Matthew, "who else could make gold out of thin air."

"An alchemist, so he-did it?" exclaimed Alexandra. "He was able to turn lead into gold?"

"Actually, that was me and Matthew, the two of us continued to tinker with father's ideas after he had given up. And it was mercury not lead," said John.

"Ach!" exclaimed Matthew. "I remember how proud he was of the two of us. His appreciation and praise meant more to me than all the gold we ever made for England." With that Matthew scooped some sand up from the deck of the ship from where he was sitting and clenched it in his huge fist. A golden hue seemed to hover over his fist and within seconds he opened his hand to reveal a one ounce ball of solid gold. "We eventually found easier ways of conjuring up gold. Mercury, of course, is poisonous."

John took the gold ball from Matthew and began to twirl it between the palms of his hands until it became a long golden string. He somehow sealed the ends together and made a necklace. He curled it over Alexandra's head. "But how...," she asked in amazement holding it in her hands as it hung around her neck.

"You mentioned that you knew my father was a theologian. Not many people know that or they dismiss it as a medieval diversion of sorts. Unlike now, back then you couldn't push the limits of authority or the sciences too far. You'd be deemed a heretic. It was a political tightrope. Fortunately, England needed gold to fight Spain and France. The discovery Matthew and I made allowed father to secure his position with the monarchy. Ultimately, it allowed him to pursue his true passion, to study the Bible uninhibited," said John.

John continued, "Obviously, Isaac is perhaps one of the most brilliant men ever born. And well, my father, just didn't read the King James Bible the version published just before he was born. He read directly from some of the most ancient texts. Many of the original texts from the third and fourth century written in Hebrew and Greek. In particular, he studied extensively not only the Book of Acts, but everything he could find on the early church. How Peter and Paul, like Jesus before them, were able to cure the sick and the lame."

John stood up from the chair and extended his hand to assist Alexandra out of her chair to stand beside him. John laid his thumb and finger of his right hand on Alexandra's eye lids and gently pushed them closed. Then removing his hand he spun her around till her back was to him and he whispered in her ear. "Now, tell me what you feel, what you hear and what you see?"

Alexandra didn't understand what he meant and shook her head with her eyes still closed. "I don't understand," she said.

As John backed away, he said, "What man has failed to grasp. What has all but been forgotten? Is the rhythm of life, it fills in all of space and time. Some physicists today call it black matter. My father called it the Holy Spirit. We, Matthew and I, call it "The Way". The Way was once the name given to the early church by the Apostles. Christianity was actually a derogatory Greek term. The Apostles referred to their movement simply as the Way."

Alexandra still couldn't see, hear or feel anything out of the ordinary. She could not believe half of what she was hearing, "John it's an incredible story. But, I'm afraid it's beyond my comprehension."

John ignored her skepticism and continued, "Alexandra, once you are touched by the Way you only have to accept its grace. Once you do, once you feel its power and accept that it exists you'll never be alone. Your every request will be granted, you'll never know fear, and you will live forever."

With John's soft voice in her ear and the soft ocean breeze blowing across the deck, Alexandra's feet gently lifted up into the air. The power of the Way wrapped her in its love and moved to heal her. As she rose several inches above the deck, her soul leaped at its touch and she accepted its grace. The prayer she had made after she was healed on the outside by the shower was answered. She was freed from the terrible memories of her kidnapping. As she floated back to the deck she fell into a deep, dreamless and peaceful restorative sleep.

chapter 7

CALCULUS

Alexandra slept late into the next day. This was after all perhaps her first good sleep since the whole nightmare began unless you count the exhaustion that had overtaken her after the trip back through time. She stretched, got out of the bunk and caught a glimpse of herself in the mirror, mirrors were one thing she had tried to avoid recently. She noted she remained completely free of her many bruises. Her face seemed almost rosy. Her eyes seemed to have some of the old twinkle. Her hair continued to look like gold and felt softer than it ever had.

Perhaps, she thought, not all nightmares as she remembered all that had taken place the day before, the dancing, the music, the incredible story John and Matthew had spun. Could it be real? What an exhilarating, indescribable and incredible feeling when she remembered how she felt when the Way, the force, lifted her off the deck of the ship. Then, just as she focused on the Way, she realized she was famished.

With energy she thought she'd never reclaim she washed, dressed and then ran up the stairs two at a time to the deck of the *Principia*. Excited to see what miracles lived in store for her this day.

As Alexandra hopped up the remaining two stairs she was greeted first by a loud caw from the Raven and then broad grins from John and

Matthew. Additionally, she was met by the cleansing breeze of cool salt air.

"Good morning my lady," said Matthew jovially.

"It's good to see you smile," added John, "And with such vitality."

Alexandra's face reddened from the attention, after all she hardly knew these two men who had spun her such a fantastic tale. "Before you tell me more. How I fit into all of this, I want to hear Matthew's and the Raven's tale." Then she added, as if she almost forgot, "Oh, and by the way I'm famished." She laughed with them as they seemed to laugh with a sigh of relief that perhaps she had lived through the worst.

Matthew smiled and said, "Ahh, a sea breeze always brings on a good appetite. As long as the seas are calm." The Raven cawed and Matthew responded to him with a chuckle, "I know you're always hungry."

John moved aside and in so doing revealed a table embellished with a small feast, white table cloth and golden place settings on display.

Alexandra's eyes widened, "You guys are amazing," she said as she, eyed the food while the aroma made her mouth water.

"The Way allows us to go without food for days and days, but it's always nice to have a good restorative feast," said John.

Matthew pulled out her chair and they all sat down to a feast of eggs, bacon, ham, fruit, rolls, pastry, tea, coffee and juice. There was even music played by an unseen musician that seemed to be timed in sync with each wave. While Alexandra ate at a pace of a woman who had not eaten in weeks John and Matthew ate at a more reasonable rate. One in which they would not choke. As they ate they all took turns being amazed by the Raven's ability to catch any morsel of food thrown in the air.

At one point when the Raven grabbed a pastry just as it was about to hit the water, Alexandra exclaimed, "Look sharks." Sure enough, a school of sharks, dorsal fins exposed, could be seen speeding alongside the vessel. "Are they dangerous?" asked Alexandra.

"Aye," responded Matthew, "Sharks are one of the few species unaffected by the shadows. Maybe because they generate such fear in and of themselves. But they're afraid of the light so they're a nice comfort to have around the ship. Gottfried as it turns out, is deathly afraid of em and therefore rarely if ever is he at sea".

"So sharks are our friends?" asked Alexandra.

Matthew and John nodded affirmatively but in hesitation. "It's sort of the enemy of my enemy is my friend," said Matthew. "They'll still happily eat us given half a chance, lassie."

"Curiously, the other species the shadows can't control are fleas," said John.

Alexandra chuckled and said "I guess, I'd prefer fleas to sharks."

Matthew nodded to John and said mysteriously, "One's as deadly as the other, and all in all, I'd prefer the sharks."

When they had eaten enough for six or seven people, and all that was left was the tea and coffee, John clicked his fingers and everything disappeared in a pinkish mist. Although Alexandra did imagine she heard everything being stowed away in the galley below.

"So," said John as everything was put away and the ship glided along in a gentle breeze, "I guess we owe Alexandra an explanation, one I need to hear as well."

The grin left Matthew's face as he became more serious. "Aye, we've some catching up to do." Matthew stood up and began to pace the deck of the ship as he spoke. "Well, as ya know John, you were captured after you operated on Pope John Paul and was able to save him after the attempt on his life."

Alexandra raised an eyebrow.

"I know," said Matthew grimacing, "Who would've thought an Anglican would save a Pope. But John here in May 1981 saved the Pope and before that in March, President Reagan. Both were shot in attempts to forestall the inevitable demise of the Soviet Union. We were in a war lassie, the Pope had to bring Poland into the mix and be supported by the United States. The entire plan depended on these men living. It had taken years and years to get them into place."

"I don't understand," said Alexandra taken aback by the scope of the pronouncement.

"We were at the time and have been ever since the seventeenth century at war with Gottfried Wilhelm Leibniz. A gentleman you've had the distinct displeasure of meeting," said John.

"Was that the man who tried to kill us in New York?" asked Alexandra.

"New York and just about every other place in the world," added Matthew.

"Perhaps," said John, "We should start a bit further back. In some respects, Gottfried Leibniz and my father have been locked in an epic struggle since the time they first met in and around 1676. I was actually about nine years old at the time. At first, my father very much welcomed Gottfried. As far as he knew, Gottfried was an advisor to the Privy counselor to the King of Brunswick. He was born in 1647 so that would have made him about the same age as my father, perhaps a bit younger, around thirty at the time. He was very bright, with an inquiring mind having graduated from Leipzig University in Saxony with a degree in philosophy and a keen interest in mathematics. Naturally, father shared his ideas with Gottfried on Calculus."

"Isaac should have written out his ideas on calculus, but instead it was Gottfried, who claimed father's ideas as his own and wrote a paper in 1693, what was it called Matthew? Something like *Supplementum Geometriae Dimensoriae* in which he claimed the authorship of calculus."

"That's right," said Matthew. "It wasn't until John, John Keil contested it in the Royal Society around 1708 that the fact even came out. But what it really all came down to was that Leibniz tried to get an appointment to the House of Hanover just before Queen Anne died in 1714. The Elector of Hanover, George Lewis of course became King George I of England. Leibniz had worked very hard to get George in position to become the English King. He was devastated to find out he would not be going to England with the new King George."

"How could he when by that time Isaac had been Master of the Mint and producing gold for the treasury for almost ten years? The new king was no fool, at least not in the early years of his reign, he needed Isaac to keep producing gold." said John.

"It turns out Leibniz banked everything on that position. He'd borrowed heavily and lived quite the high life, but without the weighty title his debtors called in their chips. Gottfried had no choice but to fake his death in 1716. The part that threw old Gottfried over the edge was that no one cared he died. Only his secretary, Remy, was at the funeral and his dead body double was forced to lie in an unmarked grave. Of course, from that point in time, in Gottfried's mind, it was war," said John.

"So all of this is about a quarrel over who invented calculus?" asked Alexandra in disbelief.

"No, not quite," said John. "You see Gottfried came back from the dead, so to speak. And somehow managed to get all my father's notes on his greatest discoveries, the philosopher's stone, alchemy and most importantly optics. You see, while Isaac was putting forth his ideas on optics in, *'A Treatise on the Reflections, Refractions, Inflections and Colors of*

Light', he was also studying The Book of Acts. One night while aligning his prisms he stumbled upon the Way, the Holy Spirit. In his prayers that night he moved a lavender light and it answered his prayers."

"And what prayer was it that was answered you may ask, my lady? It was a prayer for a cure for his seven year old son John, who'd been stricken with a case of scarlet fever," said Matthew. "His prayers were answered when a lavender light broke away from the prism's spectrum and descended onto his son and gave his son, for whom he had sacrificed so much, back his life."

There was a long pause in the story, the ship glided a bit further under cloudless skies. At last John spoke, "It was his first miracle with the assistance of the Way, the first of many. So when Gottfried stole all my father's notes he also stole his writings on the many miracles he was able to perform by praying and calling forth the many colored lights of the Way,"

"You see, Gottfried never discovered the true light of the Way, the Holy Spirit. Gottfried and his men exploit what Matthew and I call the shadows. He's never been able to tap into the light. However, by combining his sight into the shadows with others he can cause the light of the Way to be hidden from our sight. He can also manipulate the shadows in many of the same ways we use the light," said John.

"How many men does it take to hide the Way John?" asked Alexandra thinking of the multitude of men John faced down in New York City.

"A very good question," replied John. "How many clouds hide the sunshine? Like the sun the Way is always shining. However, while a few clouds can cause it to rain many clouds can hide the light completely. Further, if one calling the Way fails to display a true faith, then nothing can be accomplished with the light."

Matthew chimed in, "Unfortunately, one or two can hide the light from me, with John it usually takes four or five. It took me a long time to realize the only one who could free John from Gottfried and all his men was John himself. He was the only man who had the power to see through the fog all those men produced."

John gave out a long sigh and threw a sugar cube to the Raven, who grabbed it and flew up to the crow's nest the highest perch on the vessel. It was the only time the Raven would associate itself with anything "crows". "You see, Gottfried stole more than calculus from my father. He discovered, by gaining access to his notes, the means to manipulate some of the power of the Way. Father, and he came to the same conclusion by different means, namely, knowledge of the Way and how making use of its power should be limited. My father thought it should be only God who revealed it to individuals selected by the Holy Spirit. Gottfried, of course, wanted no one but himself to be able to fully exploit it. The men he instructs are only there to do his bidding. He by no means wants any competition for centuries it was just him and Remy. When my father, passed into the future, Gottfried attacked and has never stopped. In the end, he hopes to be the sole person with knowledge and access to the Way. If he accomplishes his goal, he will be invincible." John paused, "While Matthew, the Raven and I, and a few others have tried to stop him it has meant an endless battle throughout most of three centuries. We've been able to just barely stay ahead of him after both world wars only to be caught unaware by his twisted use of communism. He intended to unleash his spawn and start yet a third world war."

"For perhaps obvious reasons," interjected Matthew, "the shadows are stronger when humanity suffers. He uses the filth of the earth and introduces them to the shadows. The shadows love to terrorize and maim humanity."

John nodded in agreement, "It's been a long struggle and we'd just got the pieces in-place when Gottfried had both Pope John Paul and President Reagan shot. I was able to save them both in the emergency rooms posing as a local doctor. Saving Reagan had surprised them, Gottfried and his henchman. But the Pope's assassination attempt was really an attempt to capture me. As we know, it worked and Gottfried with his five well-trained henchmen were able to use the shadows, block my path to the Way and bind me to their will. They used my captivity to force my friends into the future. They couldn't kill me, I was too strong in the Way, but they were able to limit my movements and my thoughts."

Matthew spoke up, "Of course, when they captured John we tried to release him. But we also needed to continue with our plan to save the western world, so while we tried and failed to rescue John, we encouraged the Way to take out the leaders of the Soviet Union namely, Brezhnev, Andropov and Chernenko. We thought Gorbachev could be relied upon to bring about the fall and we were right. But, it came at a huge cost, while we worked on the world stage, it gave Gottfried time to strengthen his hold on John."

Alexandra was stunned into silence. She could not believe what she was hearing, "How could a man, such an evil man as Leibniz, be able to use the Way!"

"While at a much higher intensity and level, the Way is much like gravity, a law of physics. All of humanity is subject to the laws of gravity. Remember, rain falls on good and evil men. But when the Way is used for evil, it does exact a toll. You saw it's retribution in the how Remy looked."

Alexandra shuddered at the mention of his name.

"That's why one must never use the Way to directly destroy a life. Options must be provided, it must be made clear people have used their free will to select their path," said Matthew. "We can't choose a path of destruction for any life."

Alexandra shut her eyes and let the ocean breeze wash over her. "So you were captured and Matthew and the Raven tried to free you these past forty years. I wasn't even born until seventeen years ago, where do I fit into all of this?"

John looked at her intensely and said barely audibly, "We first met at your Aunt's summer palace on the Danube in 1782. The last time I saw you, was when you left London to board a ship in Southampton. You were to visit America for the first time. Although you were to travel alone we thought it'd be safer."

Alexandra felt a shiver run up her spine, she didn't know if she wanted to hear what they were saying, "My Aunt?" She asked.

"Catherine the Great," responded John.

"The Ship?" asked Alexandra.

"The Titanic "said John.

At the sound of the name of that deathly ship the Raven, screamed out loudly from above.

chapter 8

ALEXI

Alexandra's eyes flew to the bird, but John calmly told her, "Everything's fine. The Raven just takes umbrage at the mention of that ship's name. To the Raven, the name of that ship is taboo, a cursed word. Life has never been the same since the sinking of that ship. It was a turning point in all our lives."

Matthew, who was still standing was now looking out over the side of the ship. The clouds on the horizon were starting to take shape. "They're coming John, they'll be here soon."

"Aye, but before they come you have to tell me and Alexandra how she came to be in that bookstore," said John, who had risen to put his arm on Matthew's shoulder. Matthew did not turn to face John but continued to stare out at the horizon.

Alexandra was suddenly frightened. She felt a chill, but whether it was the sudden drop in temperature, the spray from the waves or the thumping on the side of the vessel by the sharks she couldn't tell. Just then the Raven flew down to sit beside Alexandra and she had to smile. Did the bird sense her uneasiness of finally being told her role in this adventure? She gently stroked his head and she asked, "What's his story?"

The Raven cawed gently as if trying to respond, "Well, we met after the Battle of Salamanca, part of the Peninsula campaign during the Napoleonic wars, around the middle of 1812. The heat that summer was intense which caused the smell from close to forty thousand dead bodies, almost three quarters, of them French, to be enough to cause most men to faint. The bodies were strewn over an area where the conflict had been waged the previous day on a broad plain. The Raven and his mate were picking over the dead. The crows liked to go for the eyes, the Raven and his mate the buttons. We, Matthew and I had been fighting in the ranks with Wellington. Gottfried had been with the French General Marmot. Matthew and I always attended to the dead after a battle, we would pray over as many corpses as we could be they English, Spanish, French or Portuguese. Gottfried was on the field of battle at the same time looking for fallen officers and their personal papers. He'd use the papers to blackmail the fallen officer's heirs. He must have cursed the crows and ravens with one deadly spell. In truth, it may have been aimed at me and Matthew. In any case, the spell hit and killed the crows on the field and it nearly killed the Raven and his mate," remembered John.

"There had been so much killing the day before, actually within those past five years. So after Gottfried left the field, when we came upon the Raven I called upon the Way and saved him. Unfortunately, I could not save his mate. The Raven, somehow when being healed by the Way, hung onto the force." The bird hopped over to John's shoulder and nudged his ear. "Ravens by nature are very smart. How he learned to use the Way, I've no clue. He's the only animal I know of that can manipulate the colors. His natural eyesight was incredible, under the Way it's been remarkably enhanced."

"He's saved our lives a dozen times over," said Matthew.

"And," added John, "Gottfried and him hate each other. So it works well for us!"

Alexandra reached out to the Raven and the bird flew down from its perch, "I think I've seen this bird before back in West Virginia."

At the mention of the term bird, the Raven hopped away. "He's very particular about how he's addressed," chuckled Matthew. Alexandra again extended her hand and the Raven hopped back over to her and almost magically appeared on her shoulder. He used his beak to play with her pearl earrings which remained from the evening before. He eyed her a moment and then nuzzled her ear.

"He likes ye lassie," said Matthew, "He don't take to just anyone. Actually, no one."

Alexandra smiled, "And you Matthew, what's your story."

"Me, I was born in Scotland, Edinburgh, to be exact, about the same year as John." Matthew shrugged his shoulders, "Not much to tell really, it was after the great fire in London that nearly burned that city to the ground. The disease, the plague, hit Edinburgh the year after. Not as bad as in London, but bad enough my mother passed. My father was a professor of mathematics at the University and he and John's father, Isaac, communicated and became friends. When dad traveled to London he took me with him and that's how John and I became friends."

"Instantly," interjected John. "It was as if we were twins. We became inseparable and were always in the thick of things. When Matthew's father passed in a sailing accident, there was no question but that Matthew should come and live with us."

"You mean study!" exclaimed Matthew, "your father put us to work and we studied nonstop for the next sixty years at his side. He is such an amazing man."

"Possibly the greatest mind that has ever existed," said John reverently.

The Raven reverently uttered a soft caw.

The mood had seemed to lighten a bit with the reciting of the Raven's and Matthew's story. However, as the Raven suggested now was the time for the difficult story. "And that leaves us only one person to discuss, Matthew," prodded John.

Matthew couldn't seem to find the words on where to start, so John broke the silence, "You see, Alexandra, we were in love, we'd been married for over a hundred years. When the Titanic sunk, when Gottfried's men pulled the iceberg into the ship's path to sink her. He made sure you were locked and sealed by the shadows in your cabin. I thought," John turned his gaze from Alexandra to Matthew. "I believed, you were lost to me for all time. My heart ached. The world slipped into the First World War and only the work of drawing the United States into the war to end it, allowed me to recover some semblance of reason and sanity. Until I saw you in the bookstore two weeks ago, I thought you were lost to me for all time."

Matthew looking out at the oncoming storm on the horizon cleared his throat and said softly, barely audible, "Well, John, Alexandra was lost to us for all time." He paused looking for the right words.

"You see, John I'd become desperate. Hooke, Wren and Halley had all failed. Whiston and Cotes just followed my orders pretty much until they too gave up and just slipped into the future after the others. They left hoping to find them all, including Isaac, and bring a solution back to me. They'd all gone into the future rather than succumb until all that was left was me and the Raven. To make matters worse, Gottfried and his men were only getting stronger not weaker. He seemed to be able to continue to expand his ranks. Then one night I said to the Raven, the only one strong enough to free you from Gottfried's curse was you yourself. And from that point on all our energy was concentrated on how we could wake you up from that bloody spell. But, how?" Matthew continued to stare out to the horizon not wanting to meet either John's or Alexandra's eyes.

John came up behind Matthew and Alexandra joined him. He placed his hand on the big man's shoulder, "How'd you do it Matthew?" asked John softly.

"I'm not sure of the ethics," said Matthew as he pulled a golden locket out from his pocket and turned to face John. "I helped Alexandra, fashion this here locket before I left on my expedition. She put a snippet of her hair into it with the intent of giving it to you on your birthday. When I looked for it years later, I realized she forgot to give it to you John. I knew she must have had it with her when the Titanic went down." Matthew handed the locket to John with a tear in each of their eyes.

John opened the locket and noticed there was no longer a hair in the center.

"There was a mission to explore the shipwreck of the Titanic. I helped fund it and was able to participate in the effort to recover valuables from the wreck. They'd developed robots with cameras that could reach the sunken vessel. She was lying under twelve thousand feet of water. Using robots, I was able to find the cabin where Alexandra had died and retrieved the locket. From the hair I," Matthew paused, "I made a clone of your ancestor, lassie. I'm sorry if I gave you false hope John, but it was the only way to bring you back."

Alexandra looked shocked, but John only nodded, he held the locket up to the sunlight and let it play with the sun's rays. Although it was not a prism the intense sunlight reflected off the gold and generated a small display of colors. "Yes," he whispered, "it was the only way."

Alexandra was stunned as she pulled away from Matthew and John walking aimlessly to the other side of the *Principia*. "I never knew my parents, of course," she said in a slow voice to herself. "But the woman that raised me... always provided for me... but she was always so cold, so distant. She said I was an orphan whom her sister had adopted, but that her sister too had passed when I was still a baby," said Alexandra almost in a trance. A tear was running down her cheek, this explains everything she thought, the benign neglect. She had always dreamed that one day she'd meet her parents, but that would never be, she had none.

The breeze appeared to turn cooler on the ship's deck. The warmth generated by the feast earlier dissipated. "I'm sorry lassie," said Matthew walking up behind her. "Once I had the DNA material, I needed a woman to give you birth. Once you were born, she wanted nothing else to do with us. I actually thought it was for the best. I found another woman to raise you and made sure you were well provided for and lacked for nothing monetarily. Obviously, I couldn't raise ye myself it was too dangerous. We, me and the Raven, checked up on ya as often as we could. You were a bonnie lassie," added Matthew.

"Cynthia, the woman you picked to raise me," Alexandra paused, "was always kind. Somehow, however, we never seemed to look at the world in the same light. She said she had no clue who my parents were and that I shouldn't dwell on it. She said I was lucky to be good looking, healthy, intelligent and blessed with the abilities to make my own life."

"That sounds cruel, but probably the best advice she could provide," said Matthew. "I purposefully kept her in the dark and had her move you from time to time for fear we'd be found out. I think she may have believed I was your father, but as you probably are aware now I couldn't risk being seen with ya. Yet, we never abandoned you, me and the Raven. You've probably seen him as a child growing up, he was often times watching out for your safety particularly when you lived on that farm in West Virginia and would go roaming the hills."

"Your father, is Alexandra's father, and he was an Anhalt Duke, who ruled Prussia in the 1800's before it was absorbed in the creation of Germany. I met him and your mother once with Alexandra. They didn't think much of my prospects or my marriage proposal. We eloped to your aunt's court, Catherine the Great's, who by the way ruled Russia for fifty years. So you are the heiress of two empires, and a woman I fell in love with and remained in love with for over a hundred years," stated John in a dreamy voice coming up to her shoulder from behind and whispering in her ear.

"Now, there was a woman," interrupted Matthew with a far off smile. "Catherine, I mean..." he added slightly blushing.

John gave Matthew a pat on the back and gave him a warm embrace. "How can I thank you for all you did for me?" asked John.

"Actually," responded Matthew with a tear running into his red beard, "I thought you'd tear my head off once you found out. I couldn't conceive of any other way to reach you John."

John gave Matthew one last pat on the back and turned back to Alexandra. He reached for her hand and when she extended it, he kissed the back of her hand. His kiss sent shivers down her spine. She wasn't quite sure why she was crying. Just that the terrible nightmare seemed to be non-stop. "I don't know how I can make it up to you. I don't know how I, or Matthew, can ever gain your confidence. We seemed to have dragged you into some nightmarish time warp, when really, you should be what, enjoying your freshman year at college?" asked John. He hesitated for a moment, then added. "You deserve your own identity would you mind if, going forward, we might address you as Alexi?"

Alexandra could hardly think her head was spinning in a hundred directions. Supposedly she was on a ship in the Caribbean some one hundred and seventy years in the past with two of the most handsome men she'd ever seen. These men were either saints or three hundred year old insane wizards. Another three hundred year old wizard, possibly aligned with the devil, wanted them all dead. And she just found out she was a clone. "Alexi," she murmured, "yes, I'd like that very much."

Matthew smiled, nodded to both John and Alexi. He seemed to relax now that the burden he had carried for so long had been thrown off. The Raven, which had circled over to Alexi hopped on her shoulder, gave her a nudge and a soft caw, the latter it seemed, was to be an offering up of his apology for going along with Matthew's crazy scheme.

Alexandra's confusion of thought seemed to affect the weather. The clouds propelled by a heightening wind rolled in rapidly, dark, heavy with rain. The wind caused the sea swells to rise dramatically. The waves rolled beneath the little ship with the whitecaps suddenly throwing saltwater into the ship and onto their faces and clothes. Lightning suddenly streaked through the air nearby, accompanied by a horrific clap of thunder. Overhead the Raven which had flown back up to the crow's nest was cawing frantically. Magically it could be heard over the thunderous storm and ocean waves.

"They're here!" yelled Matthew.

"Good. It's time to fight back!" John called as he gave a determined look toward the fast approaching storm.

chapter 9

SHARKS

"What precisely is the plan," yelled Alexi trying to make herself heard over the thunder of the ocean.

John came close to her ear and called, "We engage them and get rid of as many as we can. Then we get at least one of them to fetch Gottfried and bring him back to us in London in the year 1701."

"Simple…" added Matthew shrugging his shoulders.

Alexi, looked stunned. At first she thought she had misheard above all the noise. Why not just flee to another year, another past? Then the fear she felt at the possibility of capture struck her with a vengeance when out of the eye of the storm came three gigantic eighteenth century sailing vessels. Her knees buckled and she sat down on the deck unable to stand. The ships were massive each with over a hundred gun ports, all of which were open. They quickly got along the *Principia*, which was totally overshadowed by the three new arrivals. It was evident, even to a neophyte like Alexi, that they were using the power of the Way to control nature's forces of wind and current. The vessels all but flew into formation and sandwiched the tiny *Principia*.

In 1715, the three Spanish ships of the line had been on a mission to protect the gold fleet which sailed annually from the new world to Spain.

They had obviously been commandeered by Gottfried's underlings. Two of the vessels came up to the Principia's starboard side while the other came along the port side. The three ships combined had over one-hundred and fifty guns from the ships' broadsides pointed at the tiny vessel. Frantically looking around, Alexi noticed that their little vessel had no cannon whatsoever. This will be a very short battle thought Alexi as she was completely doused with salt water from the turbulent sea.

When the three ships pulled within a hundred feet on either side of the tiny vessel they wasted no time in releasing their full broadside of cannon. Over one hundred and fifty cannon sounded almost simultaneously. Alexi prepared for certain death. She dropped to her knees and covered her head with her arms to protect herself from what she thought with certainty would be splinters of wood. What occurred next was totally beyond her comprehension. Suddenly, there was absolute silence. It was as if someone had paused an old pirate movie while they went to fetch popcorn. The wind stopped blowing and the seas calmed themselves. She raised her head, having no idea what was taking place when to her amazement the first thing that she caught sight of were the cannon balls. They just hung in the air, as if captured in a painting, and then one by one they dropped into a calm sea, like pebbles strewn out over a pond. Alexi could actually hear them as they plopped into the water. The roar of the ocean, which only moments before seemed to announce their impending doom was now eerily silent.

Alexi smiled in disbelief and amazement, she stood up drenched in salt water and looked around for John and Matthew. Both men were standing back-to-back with their arms outstretched toward the ships. While John faced two vessels on the starboard side Matthew faced the one on the port side. Matthew's eyes were closed in concentration and his brow showed signs of perspiration. John on the other hand seemed unfazed and serene. "I could use a little help," said Matthew, just as the three vessels once again launched their full broadside only to meet the same inexplicable results.

"Of course," said John. He moved his hands together and all three Spanish ships were swept in a line facing the bow of the *Principia*. From this position they would no longer be able to offer up their broadsides. It was clear if John wanted to he could easily have sunk them all.

What power! What conceivable force was capable of moving and aligning the three huge vessels in such a fashion? Alexi went to the bow and was overwhelmed by the awesome display of power she was witnessing. As she did so, she felt her feet suddenly rise above the deck of the ship pulling her toward the recently aligned enemy ships. Just as her body was about to clear the side, she felt John's hand on her shoulder pushing her back down.

"They're calling you," said John softly. "They're trying to take you hostage."

"How?" She asked, her brow furrowed. She was tired of being manipulated and manhandled. "How can I defend myself?"

John smiled, "Reach out with your mind. The Way is strong here. It always is after a storm at sea. Nature uses the Way to calm herself. Nature prefers a state of calm, not chaos."

Alexi tried concentrating and closed her eyes in the effort, but she didn't know what to look for or what to hope to feel. At that moment John touched her cheek with the back of his hand gently moving up to her eyes. As his hand touched the corner of her eye, her knees buckled at the sight she was given. She could see waves and waves of light, like the great northern lights she had once read about, patterns of red, green and blue swirling as if a caged lion were trying to break free. "The Aurora Borealis...?" said Alexi in awe.

"Aye, that's it," said John smiling, "tell me what colors you see?"

Her gaze was out over the water, but she saw none of the ocean. "Every color imaginable, all intertwined, moving and reforming."

John was impressed Alexi could see anything, let alone multiple colors. "Try and move the blue light and set it at your feet. The blue light will stabilize you making you immune to their efforts to fly you to their ship!"

"I hardly think now is the time for an introduction to the Way," yelled Matthew, who was obviously struggling to keep the ships aligned. He appeared to be fighting ten or more of Gottfried's men as they used their sight to try and force the Spanish galleons once again to come alongside the tiny *Principia*.

When John removed his hand from the Alexi's cheek, her vision of the Way vanished. She wanted to protest, but her words got lost in her throat as she refocused her eyes and saw several members from the enemy vessels launching themselves from their ships. They were leaping into the air and flying towards the *Principia*. There appeared to be at least ten men coming towards them. Instead of splashing into the water, however, they were flying. Their hands were at their sides and they were coming very quickly.

John smiled, looked at Alexi and said, "Be calm, don't be scared. It's all..."

"I know," snorted Alexi. "It's all part of the plan." How could I ever be scared again she thought? "Besides, I could never be frightened as long as I'm by your side."

"I am," said Matthew, but he gave her a wink as he turned to face the oncoming boarders. "As you predicted," said Matthew, "Gottfried is not with them."

"Never gotten over his fear of sharks has he?" murmured John with a smile. Then he grabbed Matthew's shoulder and in a cautionary tone said, "Not yet."

Then just as Gottfried's men had all gotten about two thirds of the distance to where they were standing the Raven gave out a penetrating cry from the crow's nest.

John and Matthew each held up their arms, palms facing the approaching pirates and just like the cannonballs before all ten men were frozen in space and time. The difference this time was that Alexi could see the Way capture each man in blue light. Even without John's hand to guide her, she could see the Way! "I see it!" She cried in delight and amazement, no trace of fear in her voice.

Matthew nodded at John, and he kept his attention on the ten men suspended in midair. In the meantime, John turned his gaze towards the three vessels now all in a line in the calm sea. Alexi saw John raise his hand and direct what she saw as a yellow light enter the sea to the starboard side of each of the Spanish ships. The ocean stirred itself into an eddy, the wind rose with a roar and the three vessels were swept away back into the history from which they were borrowed.

The loss of their vessels didn't go unnoticed by the ten suspended crew members. Several cried out in shock. "You'll pay for this," cried one of the ten, "you can't let those ships just sail away. Not with what they've seen!"

"Nonsense," said John to Matthew, "they've no one to discuss it with except themselves. They're on their way to the same watery grave history prepared for them. They were part of the Tierra Firma fleet of 1715 that you and I were sent to commandeer two centuries ago. They're all overtaken by the hurricane and run aground off Florida and are never heard from again."

"Aye," said Matthew. "I actually recognize the admiral's vessel the El Capitan." He winked at Alexi, "We ran into them just before the hurricane took them out of history's pages the first time."

Alexi looked on as if to ask what that has to do with current events. Matthew continued, "We canna kill someone not of our time with the Way nor change events while we're here in our past. Otherwise, we could jeopardize our chances of ever getting back to the present."

Alexi didn't understand, but she thought now was not the time for questions. As if on cue, the wind picked up and their tiny craft moved further away from the suspended figures. Just as with the cannonballs before the men one by one began to fall toward the water. Unlike the cannonballs, however, they didn't vanish beneath the ocean. Their use of the Shadows allowed them to remain upright and stand on the water, albeit far from dry. The seas had been allowed to return to the action they were accustomed. The waves rolled through and amongst the ten figures as they regained their courage to try once again to board the *Principia* the only vessel remaining in the area.

Their courage soon departed as they were immediately surrounded by a huge school of sharks. The very same school that John and Matthew had been feeding since boarding the *Principia*. All the attackers immediately began to struggle to stay upright in the ever increasingly choppy waves. Their command of the shadows while it allowed them to walk on water would not protect them from the sharks. Alexi thought she could see a sort of scarlet mist or dome over the top of the group. She looked towards John for an explanation.

"The scarlet light you see inhibits them from leaving this day in time. They have to fight what they've brought on themselves without the ability to return to their present," explained John.

The ten men, soon just eight, were so busy fighting sharks they didn't see John take Matthew's and Alexis' hands and spin on the deck of the ship.

"To Woolsthorpe, July 15, 1701," said John calmly.

chapter 10

HOMECOMING

Once again Alexi felt like she was passing over the edge of a waterfall. The descent this time was of a much shorter duration and when they landed with a thump on wooden seats in what appeared to be some sort of stagecoach they retained consciousness. Alexi had so many questions she almost failed to notice her surroundings, almost. She found herself dressed in early eighteenth century finery. Her gown was a powder blue satiny material full length and very heavy. Her blouse came up just under her chin and she had on long white gloves that came up to her elbows. Her hair was done up in a bun and it was enmeshed in a shower of jewels. John and Matthew also were dressed in early eighteenth century attire. The coach was rocking almost as much as the vessel had in the ocean. She also noticed the smell of salt from the sea breeze had vanished and was replaced by an eye watering stable smell.

"How, where," asked Alexi in befuddlement.

"It's all part of the plan. You see lassie," said Matthew with a mischievous wink, "our plans have many facets."

"What, what will happen to those men?" she asked with concern.

"Well," said Matthew, "if we're lucky the sharks will tear them all to pieces."

"All except one," said John, "We need at least one to survive."

"Please, can you let me in on our plan!" asked Alexi emphatically with an emphasis on the word "our".

John smiled at Matthew, who said, "I thought you didn't care much for our plans lassie?"

"Well," said Alexi mischievously, "I'd at least like to know the direction we're headed so I can begin to plan my escape in the opposite direction."

"The plan," said Matthew with a fake snarl, "is to kill as many of them as quickly as possible. And to tell the truth, I wouldn't mind if the plan at some point included getting rid of Gottfried."

"I thought you couldn't kill with the Way, or you'd be permanently scarred or disfigured," questioned Alexi.

"Correct," said Matthew firmly, "We canna use the spirit to kill, but we can put our enemies in harm's way. If the shark's eat those men in the water, it's not us that killed'em. It's the sharks."

"I don't see how..." began Alexi her voice showing her frustration in trying to comprehend the rules for the new world she had entered.

"We left them options," interjected John trying to explain. "We left the ship for them to seek shelter. We left them a vision of hope."

Alexi had to consider this for a moment. Surely they knew better than she what constituted an improper use of the Way, however, it seemed to her that as with the men John killed in New York, now these men were similarly being slaughtered. "The rules seem arbitrary to me, I mean we fed those men to the sharks."

"Nae lassie," said Matthew trying to maintain his place as the coach came to quickly around a turn in the road. "Ye, have to allow people an opportunity to escape certain death. This time we left them the *Principia*.

In New York, John here offered them all peace and prosperity if they left us alone. They only had to walk away from the café."

Alexi mulled this over a moment she seemed to remember that John did offer them no harm if they walked away from the café. She remembered at the time thinking John was quite insane. They had all laughed heartily at the offer. But then coming back to their current circumstances she realized a potential flaw in the current plan, "If they make it to the ship they'll survive!"

"Aye," said Matthew.

"Oh, but if they survive won't they be able to follow us here!" This seemed like a colossal mistake in the planning process. Under no circumstances did she want to meet up with Remy, or Gottfried for that matter, ever again.

"We're counting on it lassie," said Matthew, "In fact, we left some papers in the captain's quarters that if they take the time to decode them and are determined to kill us they'll follow us here."

"But why?" exclaimed Alexi. It seemed insane to her to ever want to meet those men again.

"We give them options lassie," said Matthew softly but with finality.

As Alexi took in the meaning of Matthew's words and his tone, she realized the conversation was over. As they rode along she pondered what she had been told and she tried to apply her mathematician's logic. If those men, who somehow made it to the *Principia*, followed them here they could be killed by John and Matthew. They were, however, given options to avoid these deaths. All they had to do was walk away. Particularly after that display of power by John. What sensible man would follow them here? Alexi sat back in a huff. If there was a plan they weren't going to tell her she concluded. She was about to concede defeat when the coach went over a particularly nasty bump. "Where are we anyhow?" she demanded, "and why are we dressed like this?" After her voyage at sea, some of her old spark was returning.

Just then the carriage wheel directly below where Alexi was sitting hit a particularly deep hole in the rutted road and it propelled the lite weighted Alexi to bounce about a foot off of her wooden bench and hit her head on the roof of the carriage. John and Matthew could not help laughing. Even the Raven, which had joined them in the carriage gave a bit of a half-hearted caw. Alexi turned red and said under her breath, trying to get her composure as well as control of her many layers of garments, "You call this a plan?"

"We're on our way to Woolsthorpe, my father's estate. It's where Isaac, my father, conducted the majority of his experiments and introduced me and Matthew to the Way. There are some men there, I believe you'll find them very interesting. They are some of our dearest friends. We'll be joining them for dinner," explained John.

As he said this the coach came to a slower pace and pulled into a tree-lined lane with a distant manor house appearing in the twilight. The lane of soft crushed stone led up to a circular drive in front of the main residence. The stables which were substantial sat off to the left as the coach approached the house. There was a distinct smell of roses in the summer air and Alexi rightfully concluded there were substantial gardens nearby.

As the coach pulled up the long lane, John cleared his throat, "We're going to introduce you as Matthew's niece. Matthew and I did return for dinner at this point in our lives to Woolsthorpe in July of the year 1701 so we are in effect replacing ourselves. One more thing," and he gave a knowing glance toward Matthew, "we think it best if you lose your voice for a while. I don't think we can explain away your accent. We can introduce you as someone recovering from an esophageal inflammation."

"My voice?" shot Alexi who gave them a look of defiance. She was more upset that they would not share their plan with her.

"Yes, it'll be easier. You see Alexi we'll be among people, in particular the staff, who are very superstitious and can easily jump to the wrong conclusions regarding strangers. If you say something that might affect the flow of current and hence subsequent events, even in the slightest way, it could jeopardize our ability to return to the present," said John.

Alexi stared at John dumbfounded, she had no idea what he was talking about. She had never been particularly good at being quiet and put forth an idea of her own, "What if you introduce me as Matthew's German niece. I speak fluent German and actually Russian as well. Although, I've been told my German is better. I could pretend to be learning English. Anything I say could just be attributed to my lack of understanding the English language."

Both Matthew and John stared at her impressed. Matthew turned to John and said, "She must have inherited some of Alexandra's memories."

John looked stunned for a moment, thinking of the potential, perhaps this was why Alexi had been able to see the Way so easily on the *Principia*. "Say a few words, in German," requested John.

"Dieser seltsame traum wird immer fremde," said Alexi. (This strange dream keeps getting stranger).

"Ach, it might work," grimaced Matthew, "with that West Virginia accent, no one in Germany would understand her let alone the help at Woolsthorpe."

Alexi was about to reply, but John smiled and said, "I think it'll work, let's see, how about Matthew's Austrian cousin from Vienna. That'll make you catholic so I doubt anyone will talk to you in any case."

John and Matthew chuckled and Alexi made a face. Before she had a chance to retort the carriage came to a halt and the coachman called out "We're here my lords."

"Ah, just in time for supper," said Matthew rubbing his hands together.

While Matthew paid the coachman and distracted him with conversation, John helped Alexi out of the carriage from the other side and hurried her down the path. After all, three hundred and twenty years ago the coachman had not seen a lady, a beautiful young lady dressed in blue satin, climb aboard his coach in London. Nor had he seen all the luggage which the staff at Woolsthorpe needed to see for such a distinguished visitor from Vienna. John had the baggage materialize once they reached the door, as it was less to carry.

To Alexi's credit, she only tripped on her long gown twice walking up to the entrance. There the servants greeted Master John and Master Matthew warmly and even made a fuss over Alexi, at least until it was whispered she must be Catholic. They asked after Master Isaac, who they told the staff had remained in London hard at work. Alexi was introduced to several of the young female servants who would see to her comfort and suggested she might like to freshen up before dinner. The cook was told to add three more for dinner as they were all excited to tell John and Matthew that five of their friends were already at the dinner table.

Of course, John and Matthew knew their friends would be sitting down to dinner as they had been several hundred years earlier. The first time, however, they had not been accompanied by Matthew's beautiful young Austrian cousin.

When Alexi walked into the dining room with Matthew and John they entered a huge hall where five men were all earnestly engaged in discussing the news of the day, the Act of Settlement, which now required the King or Queen of England to be Protestant. When they noticed Alexi all conversation came to a halt and she saw five jaws drop in silence. They were stunned by Alexi's beauty, a beauty that John and Matthew had started to take for granted. There was something about her bearing, the long golden hair and emerald eyes of the twenty first century young female that caught everyone at the table off guard.

All the men were full of compliments and Alexi not use to the chivalrous manners of the early eighteenth century could only smile and blush from all the attention. She could understand what they were saying, but just barely. The old English was hard on her West Virginia ears, almost as hard as the New York City accent had been when she first matriculated to Columbia University.

It actually took the group a moment to even notice John and Matthew they were so overwhelmed by Alexi. As they regained their composure, they greeted both men heartedly and as they did so they all stood up and bowed toward Alexi. An older gentleman approached her, bowed, reached for her hand and kissed the back of it. He said, "Madame, we've been waiting quite some time for our friends to finally arrive. We were beginning to get very upset at them for their tardiness. Needless to say they are forgiven as we had no idea they were out kidnapping angels!"

All the men roared in agreement. Matthew put on a look of seriousness and said, "Alright, alright, calm down you bunch of pagans. This here's my niece from Vienna, on her way to visit my Aunt in Edinburgh. Ye've to forgive her as she knows just enough English to be misunderstood! But I already warned her about your poor uncouth manners." This comment brought on a roar of denunciation from the five men and smiles all around from the staff setting the table and starting to fill it with food.

The same man that had charmingly kissed her hand said, "If she's hanging around with you two she obviously will learn little of the Queen's language with the exception of clever curse words."

Once again the group roared with laughter and approbation. Alexi could not help but display a truly marvelous smile which made her, if possible, even more beautiful. The man, obviously smitten, smiled and introduced himself, "My lady, my name is Sir Robert Hooke, and you may call me Hooke." As Sir Robert bowed Alexi performed what she thought was an adequate curtesy. Hooke taking her hand and leading her away from Matthew proceeded to introduce her to the other gentlemen in the room. Hooke, a man in his early sixties led her to another man of approximately the same age and introduced him as Sir Christopher Wren. He continued onto Sir Edmund Halley, a man in his mid-forties. A Master William Whiston, a younger man in his late thirties and the youngest man in the group Master Roger Cotes who appeared not yet to be twenty years of age and hence closest in age to Alexi.

Cotes was so smitten with Alexi, as to be so tongue-tied to the point he couldn't even pronounce his own name. This really got the group fired up and prompted John to say, "You have to forgive poor Cotes, my father rarely lets him leave his books."

Alexi although obviously never having met any of these men before was stunned that she had heard about all these men, in her studies. Hooke and Wren were both famous polymaths and architects the latter would go on to build St. Paul's cathedral and design over sixty churches. Halley would map a comet and have it named for him. While Whiston and Cotes were two of Isaac Newton's most celebrated students. Alexi did her best curtsy as she met and accepted each man's kiss on the back of her hand. John could tell all of them were smitten and when he suggested

Alexi might be tired and need to retire to her room. All five men declared in unison that John should retire, but Alexi should stay.

It was one of the most charming and interesting evenings Alexi ever had the occasion to partake. All the men were geniuses, despite them only having knowledge of events and discoveries leading up to the year 1701, they discussed topics ranging from optics to architectural problems to alchemy as well as the politics of the day. The Spanish, the French, and even the Hapsburgs in Austria, with a nod to Alexi. Alexi might as well have been a mute for despite her twenty-first century knowledge she had little to nothing to add to the conversation. Throughout the evening each man jested and insulted the others only to be applauded for the better insult. It was obvious to her that these seven men were the best of friends and as she was to find out each would gladly sacrifice their lives to save one another.

For their part, John and Matthew, both participated in the far ranging topics. She could tell while all the men respected each other they truly hung on every word from John. With John's father off in London, it was John they all turned toward. For some reason, John kept trying to steer the conversation to medical trials and vaccines. Meanwhile, all Hooke, Halley and Wren wanted to discuss was Alexi's safety by which they suggested it would be much better if they accompanied the young Austrian to heathen Scotland themselves. As it was part of the plan all along, after they persisted for the appropriate amount of time, Matthew agreed Alexi should stay here at Woolsthorpe and enjoy their company for the next several weeks.

Of course, from Alexi's perspective, there was another benefit from the gathering that evening. There was a hearty display of eighteenth century cuisine and she was famished. The array of meat dishes was overwhelming including; venison, pigeon, sirloin of beef, turkey, duck, partridge and what she was told was chyne of mutton (lamb). There were no vegetables or fruit for which Alexi felt a sudden craving, but then there were some delicious varieties of wine. Her cup remained full after every sip. At first she thought it might be some of John's magic, but she noticed it was just Hooke forever filling her cup. Being just seventeen, even in her own time, in her own world, she had never had much of an acquaintance with alcohol. As the evening wore on, she felt very relaxed but also became very wary. This was after all not her world, not her time, and she did not feel completely at ease despite the friendliness of John's and Matthew's friends. She was wary of the staff that kept popping in and out of the great hall unannounced and for the most part unacknowledged. She didn't want to in any way, let Matthew or John down and say something that would cause a problem.

At last she was so overwhelmed she had to beg Matthew to lead her to her room in what was her best tipsy West Virginian German accent. All the men except John and Matthew objected vociferously. However, after many bows, curtsies and a few more toasts, she was led out the banquet room and up the stairs by Matthew. The discussions she could tell were just getting serious. As she left, she was surprised to notice Halley playing with what looked like a pair of dark goggles. She was about to comment when she caught John's eye and thought it best to ask later.

As the maid led them down the hall, Matthew whispered to Alexi in German with a distinct Scottish accent, "You seem to have made quite an impression lassie."

Alexi smiled, noticed the maid listening, and responded in German, "Danka, Onkel, they were most flattering. Are all your English friends so enamored with Austrian women?"

"Actually," said Matthew with a wink, "Any lassie."

Alexi noticed the maid that had accompanied them smile, and she realized that at least one of the servants spoke German.

As the door to her room was opened, Matthew bowed and went back down the hall, her chamber maid appeared and helped her into her nightgown and she quickly fell into the largest and most comfortable feather mattress she had ever imagined possible. Whether it was the feather bed or the amount of wine consumed once her head hit the pillow she slept until the morning light tickled her eyes.

chapter 11

THE WAY

The following morning Alexi stayed in bed as long as possible. She didn't want to leave the warmth of the feathery mattress. The morning brought a beautiful blue sky that peeked through the drawn curtains. She had slept so well and it was so comfortable she had little trouble convincing herself it was best to stay right where she was as it had to be the safest place. No blood, no sharks, no being injected with unknown drugs. Why ever get up, she asked herself. Before she could provide herself an answer, however, there was a knock at her door and in popped the maid that had helped her unpack her things and get into bed late last night.

"Lady Alexi," the maid bowed slightly, speaking very slowly in old English hoping to be understood by the Austrian catholic, "Master John was hoping to escort you around the gardens after you had a bite to eat."

Alexi, pretended she didn't understand and had the maid go through several more iterations before she acknowledged her meaning. After she washed and dressed and while she ate a delicious pastry washed down with a cup of tea, a second maid popped in and asked if she could braid Alexi's hair in an English style. Alexi consented gladly and as her hair was being prepared Alexi engaged the woman in a brief conversation in halting

English. The maid said her name was Bertha and that she was new to the staff at Woolsthorpe. She claimed she was so excited to be at the house of the famous Isaac Newton. She asked Alexi several questions about her travels, but Alexi thought it best to act as if she couldn't understand. Alexi thought the woman a bit forward for a servant, but thought not much more about it as she had little experience with what was a proper or improper servant in the eighteenth century. Afterwards, Bertha led Alexi to John, who was waiting patiently in the gazebo overlooking the vast gardens.

"I see you figured out how to dress as an eighteenth century Austrian princess. I'm sure it wasn't easy," said John smiling ruefully while escorting her down a path of crushed stone between carefully manicured high hedges and rose bushes of every imaginable color.

"Actually, it's very strange, it all seems familiar to me somehow. Bertha did provide me a lending hand as well," she said in a hushed voice as Bertha was nearby. The Raven greeted Alexi with a happy caw and the maid skittered away quickly.

"Bertha, who's Bertha," asked John amused.

"The servant lady who did my hair. Do you like it?" She asked turning around.

John was so happy to see her in such a good mood he asked no further question about the maid. He was intrigued by something Alexi had said. "You mentioned some of this seems familiar to you. Besides the corset, anything else?"

She smiled, "I don't know who invented the bra, but we women of the twentieth century owe him, or her, a debt of gratitude. But yes, many things seem familiar why even these grounds, these roses, this path seems familiar to me. Does that make any sense?"

John stopped and could not help but display his astonishment. "Perhaps Matthew's process captured more than Alexandra's beauty and charm, maybe it brought along some of her memories. I introduced Alexandra to the Way, here in this very garden in the late 1780's." He paused as if the memory hurt him deeply, then continued, "When I first saw you, back in the bookstore, for the first time, I thought you were Alexandra. I think that was the shock Matthew and the Raven were hoping for. After we escaped your lack of knowledge as to who or what I was confused me, but I thought it was either the spell they'd put on me. Or Matthew had used a spell to disguise you as a younger Alexandra, and had erased your memories to get you passed all the guards. I concluded you were unable to see me properly, to know me until perhaps both of us was somehow fully restored." He paused, shaking his head, "I've to keep reminding myself that you are not Alexandra. The fact that you have so many of her characteristics and memories makes it very difficult. But yes, Alexandra and I visited these grounds many times. After Isaac moved on, I was able to keep the manor house and grounds in various names. So if you've retained some of her memories than I'm sure this is one that would be at the forefront as this is one place she loved above all others. It was for the most part of our time together our home."

Alexi spun around taking in the beauty of the gardens. "I'm not sure if this is her memory, but I find it absolutely amazing," her smile said as much.

John cleared his throat and then it seemed, somewhat nervously said, "As we look toward the future." He paused briefly and then continued, "Well, what I mean to say is, if you're interested. I'd like to provide you some lessons in the manner of the Way. Frankly, Matthew and I could use the help, and we think you would be a particularly fast learner. Obviously, it's very dangerous, but if you're interested, well, at the minimum we need you to be able protect yourself until we can restore you back to your classes at Columbia."

The moment John began, Alexi had caught her breath and her heart, after skipping a beat, had begun to beat very rapidly. For a moment she thought, she hoped, John meant to talk about them, their future together. But as she focused more on what John was saying, she nodded, "Yes, of course I'd like to help. I'd love to learn more." The truth is, the past few weeks, she had just been focused on just trying to survive. The thought of returning to her classes someday never even entered her mind until John mentioned it.

"Good, I want to try and introduce you to the Way in a sort of a crash course. If, as we hope, you've retained some of Alexandra's memories the learning curve should be significantly shortened. Alexandra was very strong in certain areas of the Way, particularly in healing the sick and the maimed, let's see."

They had walked away from the manor house over a slight hill which put them out of sight of the servants. The Raven was circling overhead and gave John an all clear caw that they were indeed alone. John reached out and lightly touched Alexi's temple. "Tell me what you see?"

Alexi, sucked in her breath as the colored lights that she had seen on the *Principia* returned and swirled all around her and John. The colors were so vibrant they put the roses to shame. "Colors!" exclaimed Alexi laughing with delight, "every color imaginable a hundred rainbows. As if I'm in a room with a thousand prisms. They're all swirling and dancing," she smiled a brilliant smile that took John off guard.

"But, John how is this even possible? Where does all this energy even emanate?" asked Alexi in awe and wonder. "What are the lights, what do they represent?"

It was evident that John anticipated these questions because he pulled a piece of chalk from his pocket and handed it to her. "Do you remember Isaac's formula for gravitation that I edited in your textbook?" asked John. "The one that had Professor Horowitz all flummoxed."

Alexi accepted the chalk and bent down upon the path as she drew the ankle length dress around her. They had been walking down a path of flagstones and she wrote on a large stepping stone;

$$F = ((Gm1/m2)/r^2) \ (Ą+\Omega+\psi) \ ^3$$

"I know what the first part of the equation means, of course, it's from your "*Principia*", it's the law of universal gravitation. Every particle in the universe is attracted to every other particle by a force proportional to a product of their masses and inversely proportional to the square of the distance between them," Alexi said authoritatively. "Still, I've no idea what the last factor means."

"Alexi, with all that you've experienced since we met and your shared memories. All that you know about Isaac's theological studies, what comes to your mind when you focus on the last half of the formula?" asked John.

Alexi stood and studied it carefully for several minutes without speaking before saying slowly in a whisper, "I am the Alpha and the Omega, the beginning and the end. I will give to the one who thirsts from the spring of the water of life without cost."

John looked relieved and said, "That's right, The Book of Revelation chapter 21 verses 6 and 7. He who overcomes will inherit these things. To understand, to see and make use of the total spectrum of the Way, you have to be capable of accepting the grace Jesus offered. Solomon, Professor Horowitz, was Jewish and despite his great mind, he never read the New Testament. He was never called and I felt I couldn't explain these things to him."

"You see," continued John, "Isaac found through John's Gospel words which explained that the power of the Way is available to all who seek and it's provided without cost. You only have to ask for the many gifts offered by the Holy Spirit. Like gravity the Way is available to all, but Isaac felt these extraordinary gifts were meant to be bequeathed or taught only to a selected few. Not those simply chosen by Isaac or myself, but those selected by the Holy Spirit. Once chosen, you may either train yourself with the knowledge the Spirit provides or seek other counsel and guidance. Isaac, of course, taught himself and then everyone you shared dinner with last night. Once blessed with the knowledge of the Way, once you accept its gifts, you become endowed with an extraordinary power. Ultimately, it's a power to be used to help others less fortunate than yourself, those still seeking. The Way is here to respond to your every need, you only have to ask. The only condition is that you never use the powers of the Way to directly harm life or inflict pain. If you accept this one condition, then the Way seems prepared to accept you as I am prepared to guide you upon what is an incredible journey."

Alexi took in everything John said and she realized the precious gift being offered to her. She could only nod and stammer, "Yes, of course."

John smiled, "There's so much to learn. It's important not to let yourself be overwhelmed. Try and absorb everything and don't hesitate to ask questions." Even John had to smile at this last suggestion as he could tell Alexi was not one to hesitate in questioning authority.

"I was raised Baptist," said Alexi in a hurried tone. "My mother, I mean the lady Matthew selected to raise me, always took me to church every Sunday. She seemed to want to find an Anglican church, but there were very few in West Virginia," Alexi added nervously. "I thought it odd all those years because I never felt she believed in the church. I realize now she never believed. Matthew must have made her take me to church on Sundays a condition of payment."

John smiled, "I'm sure Matthew would have made it a requirement, but it's not about the sect or even purity of thought, it's about being called by the Holy Spirit to help others hear and understand His word." John bent down and took the chalk and circled the older part of the formula, "So, just as the force of gravity is mathematically determined and fixed. Isaac found that the force of the Way is fixed, determinable and indeed measurable. He identified three elements of the way; alpha, omega, and epsilon. The alpha is the red light, omega the blue and epsilon the yellow, the primary colors. The light, the color, we choose from those provided to us by the Way is a mixture of the three primary colors. The energy identified and used by us, is the selected light's wavelength which, when cubed provides nature's perfectly balanced equation. The energy of the Way allows us to manipulate and alter the physical world. You might say that gravity holds everything down while the Way holds everything up. As the Way is a force of nature like gravity itself, anyone can access this power. However, without guidance, even if one can see the lights, it can take years and years before a person can guide and make use of the power. Some lights seem to allow for simple transformations. Gold, for instance, allows for the transformation of any substance into gold. Silver would be the same. Red's a bit tricky, but as you've seen red allows clothing to be altered or even sails to be mended. Alexandra was a master of the violets and especially lavender as they allow the caller to heal. You've experienced the healing and calming effects of the lavender mist. Then of course there're the shadows, or the lessor colors, they allow for physical or fundamental shifts such as time travel and longevity of life itself. There appear to be as many colors as there are needs. It's even more complex, however, because a person's personality, the caller's relationship with the Spirit, seems to affect which colors may be called and subsequently used. Different people have different strengths and weaknesses within the Way,"

"You've mentioned the shadows before," commented Alexi. She was so enthralled and wanted to learn everything.

"Yes, that's right. Matthew and I refer to the edges of the light as the shadows. Perhaps you'll remember James chapter one verse seventeen. *Every good and perfect gift is from above, coming down from the Father of the heavenly lights, who does not change like shifting shadows.* Obviously, the shadows include the section of the spectrum from black to gray, but also the darker colors at the edge of the primary colors like dark purple as it fades to navy blue. The shadows provide the foundation for all the other colors and while we can and do use the shadows, we believe Gottfried can't see or use the brighter colors. He's limited to the basic colors while he has no idea of the full power the entire spectrum of the light has to offer. His soul, so dense in evil, has no hope of ever enjoying the true beauty of the entire Way. The lights making up the shadows are very difficult to manipulate and control. Ultimately, their function tends to vary ever so slightly from day to day and user to user. On the other hand, the brighter lights, once learned, are easy to call upon and fixed in nature."

John paused, "Gottfried's men probably have been shown an even smaller spectrum in which to operate. However, despite their limitations they are much more powerful than ordinary men. And the understanding and access to even just a fraction of the shadows allows them a lengthy life. Unfortunately, one or two with even limited training can cause a significant disruption in the Way, almost like static in a radio wave or a very thick cloud cover. This was how they held me in captivity all those years, denying me access to the light while keeping me in a weakened condition. When you rescued me in the bookstore his men overreacted in such a fashion that even those untrained in the Way could see its power. Normally, the shadows are not able to be seen. The lights or the colors of the Way, however, want to be seen and will actually leave a trace. You may have seen a rainbow in the sky and your scientific mind may think it merely a reflection of the refraction and dispersion of light in water droplets. That indeed may be all that it was, but it may also have been a trace left behind by someone powerful who used the Way in an amazing display of God's love."

John and Alexi continued to a spot overlooking a small pond. As she gazed at the sunlight reflecting off the water. It seemed to him, at that moment, that her youthful fascination was as beautiful as the Way itself. As Alexi gazed at the colors of the Way playing joyfully around them John spoke softly, "I'm not sure how Isaac found this spot. But somehow he was able to calculate that this spot in this garden at this time of year drew the Way in a particularly vibrant fashion. Ultimately, this was the place where he introduced Matthew and me to the Way. It was also from this spot at this time of year that I introduced Alexandra. Tell me can you see a yellow light?" asked John.

"Oh, yes," said Alexi, "but it's more of a gold than yellow, I think."

"Perfect," said John and he plucked a small rose bud off of a nearby bush. He placed the rose in Alexis' hand. "See if you can cajole, think the gold light to encircle the rose in your hand."

Alexi thought at first this would be an impossible task. It would be like using your mind to capture a butterfly or move a flame. However, as she focused, as she concentrated, the gold light actually reacted to her mind's eye and it came to rest over the rose bud she held in her palm. The golden light seemed to begin to vibrate from within the rose bud.

John too could see the gold light hover above the rose. He said to Alexi, "Close your eyes and concentrate on how the rose would look if it were solid gold." Alexi did as requested and after a few moments John said, "Now, open your eyes."

When Alexi opened her eyes the first thing she noticed was that the lights of the Way had vanished from her palm. As her focus switched from the absence of lights to the rose she gasped. The rose bud had turned to solid gold. The petals gleamed very brightly and the former rose bud had become quite heavy. "Did I do that?" she asked in a soft voice.

John smiled, "Indeed, Matthew and I discovered the use of the golden light the same way as you just used it. We in turn showed it to Isaac, who was greatly relieved we wouldn't have to form a monopoly in mercury. It's where he is now off in London as the Master of Mint making gold for Queen Anne," said John.

"Making gold?" asked Alexi.

"Yes, it's actually an interesting story. It seems we can't steal enough from the new world or from the Spanish fleet. Therefore, Isaac offered up to Queen Anne and subsequently to George to create more wealth as long as no one asks how. He told them the secret to a great economy was great coinage. In the past, coins were continually chipped along the edges so that at each use of the coins in a transaction a little less gold was passed on. He suggested that by properly minting the coins with slots already on the edges the coins wouldn't be defaced after each transaction. This would in turn provide confidence in the realm's coins. This requires, of course, that all the old coins be collected, the gold melted and ultimately used to make new coins. As he makes the new coins he triples the amount of gold materializing in the form of new coins. England has become richer than Spain."

"I can't believe it," Alexi chuckled, "I always wondered how England competed against the Spanish gold mines in the Americas. And no one questions where all the gold is coming from?" She said this as she admired and twirled the golden rose in her hand.

"Well," John laughed, "no one questions success. Of course, Isaac has to be careful not to produce too much gold or the economy would over heat."

That afternoon as they walked back to the manor house, John slowed his pace and said, "I'm very impressed you were able to move and control the golden light of the Way so quickly. In our world this is really advanced. It would compare to, say, advancing to the fourth year of physics at Columbia upon arrival at the University. It's something that normally takes years to accomplish."

Alexi nodded and smiled at the compliment as she held up the golden rose. "But," said John. "I need you to put on your physics hat on once again. As you know, the visual light we see with our eye travels in wavelengths of approximately 400 to 700 nanometers. But once we go beyond the visual array there are radio waves, infrared, ultraviolet and of course x-rays. The Way encompasses all these wavelengths in its spectrum."

"I can't imagine ever being able to comprehend all of this," said Alexi shaking her head.

"I only bring this up now so that you have some comprehension of the full scope of the Way's power. The visual light is primarily used to manipulate the physical world around us. Use of the ultraviolet rays when pulled through a person's mind allow you to manipulate that person. You can change how they act or when necessary cause them to forget. I had to use this on Professor Horowitz and a couple of other men once after we first met. If you feel a draw upon your mind you can use the orange light of the visible spectrum to protect yourself."

Alexi, nodded in disbelief. Seeing her disbelief, John said, "Let me demonstrate." John called upon the Way and using the ultraviolet ray had Alexi trip and fall into his outstretched arms.

She looked a bit taken aback, "Why my mind just went completely blank I couldn't remember how to even walk."

"You have to be careful," said John helping her regain her balance. "It only takes a slight touch of the ultraviolet rays. You can read people's thoughts as well, but you must be careful as you can cause serious damage if you linger too long."

"What are some of the other uses?" questioned Alexi.

"One use of x-rays that you've seen allows one to freeze time and in so doing freeze the actions of those around you, in effect you can stop the flow of time," responded John. "You experienced this first hand when we evaded the bus."

This got to be too much for Alexi, her head already spinning, "John, however, did you learn to use all of this?" Alexi asked.

John smiled, "Well, I had a good teacher, of course, Isaac. Then there was Matthew and all the guys you met here at Woolsthorpe. I can remember Isaac and Hooke having drawn out fights over whether light traveled in particles or waves. Hooke turned out to be right, of course, light travels in measurable waves. It was with this knowledge that they were able to develop the formula we discussed earlier. A variation in the combined wavelengths of the three primary colors of just ten nanometers seems to allow for a different use or function within the spectrum. We've never stopped experimenting and learning, and finally, it became necessary to develop knowledge to fight Gottfried just to stay alive."

A few days later as they proceeded to walk down the garden path near the spot where Alexi had managed to turn the rosebud to gold, John took Alexi by the elbow and turned her to him so that she was looking up into his flashing blue eyes. "We need to discuss something else that's very important, but I don't want you to become frightened at what it might mean. It's just a precaution really. But, now that you've demonstrated that not only can you see the Way, but have the ability to manipulate the lights, it makes sense, we be prepared for any possible danger." Alexi had learned so much and had experienced such enjoyment in the gardens with John these last few days that she was having trouble focusing on what John was trying to tell her. What danger could possibly exist for her or him with the power and beauty of the Way available to them and its willingness to grant them their slightest request?

John hesitated, "Alexi, as I mentioned to you, my wife Alexandra, was very powerful in certain areas of the Way, I think it's obvious you've retained much of her knowledge and memory. But what I have to ask you is," John paused yet again as what he had to ask Alexi was necessary but very difficult for him. They sat down on a bench overlooking the small pond.

"John," encouraged Alexi, "just ask?"

"Can you look back, back in your memories and see if you can see a ship?" asked John hesitantly.

"The Titanic?" asked Alexi.

"Yes," said John, "you see if we get separated. If something goes awry with our plan."

"What could go wrong with your bloody plan," smiled Alexi in a teasing voice. A plan she had yet to be told.

"Yes, exactly," said John, "If we ever become separated I need you to get back to that dock. The White Star shipping company in Southampton.

I was unable to be there when the ship left Southampton at noon 10 April 1912. I know, however, that Alexandra would have been looking for me from the deck and I know it would've been emotionally devastating for her that I wasn't there. If I'm correct, you'll have experienced this vision before in your dreams growing up as a child."

Alexi was a bit shocked she'd never told anyone of her dream. "Yes," she stated in a trembling voice. "When the dream comes to me, I'm always so scared, so anxious. It must be the memory you want to know about."

John nodded in relief, "No, I think I know all that I need to know about that day. The thing is it's easier to make a solo jump in time if it's linked to an emotional event in your past, it guides you to the point in time you're seeking. You see, if we ever get separated, I need a place only you and I know of, a place in time we can both reach safely. If needed, that's where I can find you. It would be like the island we escaped to from New York. It's the place Matthew, the Raven and I experienced in the past together and arranged as a place to meet if we get separated."

Alexi was very still for a minute, then said, "Even, if as you suggest, it's a place we both recognize. How would I ever get there?" Alexi had become quite frightened by John's tenor. Her sense of safety depended on John and all that she had been recently taught. She wondered if it was even possible that a memory could be wired into her DNA and be strong enough to guide her through time.

"The Way will show you the right light to call, it's a soft blue-gray mist. Pull it toward you and concentrate on the pier and the date. I'm sure it's the same event in time," said John.

Alexi was a bit scared it seemed terribly unlikely that she would be able to move in time to a place she'd never been. "I'm not sure I'm capable of such a leap John."

John paused and swallowed with difficulty from emotion, "It was, perhaps, the most traumatic event in my life. We were very much in love and I was very afraid for Alexandra's safety. Gottfried was gaining such a tremendous amount of power over the new Kaiser in his homeland while I was losing my influence here and in France. As we now know, the world was just a few years from being thrown into the First World War. We possessed no idea the dark days of 1912 were about to become so bloody. That moment in time is etched in my memory. I'm sure it was in my wife's as well, perhaps one of her last memories which is why it would be so prominent in your DNA. You've no idea of the tremendous skills you inherited. What you did these last few days is incredible. Why it took Matthew and me years to learn what you've grasped innately. It took Alexandra years as well…" A tear formed in John's eye, but he would not let it fall.

"I'm so sorry for your loss John," said Alexi and she realized that her tears once begun would not stop.

"I'm sorry Alexi," John sniffled, "only moments ago your smile was brighter, than the Way." He pulled out a handkerchief and wiped away her tears. "If we become separated and it comes at a time of need, you'll have to call the blue-gray light of the Way and while concentrating on that pier pull the light around your body. I'll come to you as soon as I can. We should practice at least once before the time, God forbid, you need to try it alone."

"I'd like to give a try, but I must admit I'm exhausted from today's training and there's a question I've been dying to ask you." She said this as she wiped away her tears. "John, none of this would be necessary if not for Gottfried. Why does he hate you so much? Why does he dislike the world so much?" asked Alexi.

Of all the questions Alexi may have asked, John had least expected this question. He shrugged his shoulders, John had taken Gottfried's hatred as a fact of life another formula carved in the laws of physics. "My father is not the easiest man to love. He's brilliant, brilliant beyond compare and that intellect can't bear to be besmirched or deemed lesser than any other. Isaac's ego has gotten him into more trouble than he cares to admit," John smiled. "Gottfried and Isaac were of the same ilk, they share the same ego. Although, Gottfried is more of a copier or a meddler than an original thinker, he is brilliant. In the end, if they were within shouting distance of each other they were shouting."

John thought for a moment and tried to think of one of a thousand events that would best exemplify the disparity and hostility between the two men. "When my father was thought to pass away, in 1727, his casket was borne by three Earls, two Dukes and a Lord Chancellor. When Gottfried had to fake his death in 1716 it was to escape debtor's prison. His body double was placed in a potter's grave with only an ex-secretary, Remy, to see to his burial. None of the orders he formerly belonged to even acknowledged his passing. He blamed everything on Isaac and the debate over the origins of calculus. Truth be told, Isaac would have boastfully taken credit."

"After my father slipped into the future and as Gottfried approached the age for his natural death, he was somehow able to steal and decode my father's diaries. From these he was able to make contact with and control the shadows of the Way. It infuriates him even more that the Way hides its true colors from him, a fact to this day he refuses to acknowledge," added John.

Alexi felt she started to understand, "It explains a great deal about their enmity. But where did your father go? You said he slipped into the future? Yet, you say he didn't die? Can't he help us?"

"Unfortunately, no," said John emphatically. "My father lived an incredible life, by 1727 he was already eighty-five. He feared people were beginning to suspect the truth that he'd indeed found the philosopher's stone. How to make gold and how to extend life. If people realized you could create gold the world's economy would crumble. If men realized they could live forever," John paused and chuckled, "well let's just say most men deserve to pass within their allotted time set by God. In any case, Isaac decided he would fake his death and try stepping into the future. From the future he hoped he could see the impending problems and correct them before they struck mankind. Or in a sense, find the vaccine the future developed before the disease could spread in the present."

"The future, didn't you say it was impossible to go forward in time," asked Alexi.

"It's not impossible to go forward, you simply encase yourself in azure, or the sky blue light of the Way. The color you'd see the sky appear from a mountain top on a clear cool morning. However, once you slip into the future, as far as I know, it's nearly impossible to find your way back."

John reached out and touched Alexi's golden hair. The maid had braided it for her in the same fashion as on their first day in the gardens. "Time is much like a braid of hair. A braid is made up of thousands of hairs. The events of billions of people all woven into one point in time. It's not difficult to find where a hair starts in the braid, its root in the past. What we call the present, the main thrust of time is like the braid itself, strong, thick with billions of strands woven together made up by the unique events of the past. The present is at the tip of the braid waiting to grow further. The past has woven itself into the present. When we go back in time, it's possible to alter the past and if we do, we'll live out a future apart from everyone else which had already been formed in the old braid. Our new destiny would take place in a newly formed braid. It's for that reason when we travel in the past, we have to be careful our adventures don't lead us down a different path, an alternate braid. As such, when we slip into the past, we have to be extremely careful to limit our contact with as few people as possible. Otherwise, we risk changing their future and ours. I mentioned x-rays to you the other day. Gottfried and his men are very good at using x-rays, especially when it comes to momentarily freezing time. Remy used this on the subway car and Gottfried in the café. You can block out any interference from day to day events and it allows you to jump right back into the present. It's much safer than jumping back in time, even for a few moments. Gottfried's a master of the shadows. Fortunately for us, he's not particularly strong in time travel, you need a touch of the lighter blue light."

Seeing Alexi about to draw the wrong conclusion John added, "Oh, they can travel back in time, just not in a very precise manner. To find us they have to scatter all their resources through time looking to find us in places they know we've been before. They can't use a simple trace."

"Your analogy of the braid helps a great deal explaining the past and present. Can you use it to explain the future?" Alexi queried.

John nodded, "The future is, of course, yet to be made. Hairs yet to be grown. It's virtually impossible for any man, even it appears for Isaac, to see which of the many paths provided by the future could take one back to the current main braid of the present. There are just too many variables, too many intangibles." Seeing one of Alexi's hairs brushed onto to her sleeve that very morning, John pulled it off and said, "Can you put this hair back into your head from whence it was pulled?"

Alexi shook her head and smiled, "Of course not."

"Trying to travel from the future back to the present is like trying to trace back the origin of a single hair from whence it was released.

Perhaps, only God can travel the whole spectrum of time. Although, there was one instance where Matthew and I think Isaac may have made contact with us. So from time to time we'll leave notes for him hoping he can use them to track us down to our present," concluded John solemnly.

Alexi tried to take this all in, "So you intend to take us back, back to the point in time we left. What you call the present?" She felt her whole body shiver at the thought. For some reason she felt safe in the past, here with John, Matthew and the Raven. To go back to New York City, to the café, she feared would mean she would have to face all that pain again and try to overcome her fear.

"It's God that determines our path Alexi. He sends us toward our future knowing that there is no obstacle we can't surmount with the help of the Way," John smiled and stroked the side of her face. "I think His plan for you is to return to the present and help lead others to Him."

Alexi and John spent a whole incredible week in the gardens of Woolsthorpe. Sometimes Matthew accompanied them and put his Scottish spin on his relationship with the Way. The Church of Scotland, or Kirk, was his bedrock. But most of the day from morning till evening it was just the two of them in the gardens with John continually coaxing Alexi to engage and better understand and manipulate the Way. The Raven remained throughout their wanderings in the garden high overhead ever circling, ever watchful. In the evening, every evening, they had dinner with John's and Matthew's incredibly intelligent, kind and hilarious friends. She felt like she truly was Matthew's niece from Venice. It was, thought Alexi, the most beautiful days of her life. When she entered the conversations her knowledge of physics and mathematics allowed her to fit in and contribute to the stimulating conversations. She was careful not to offer up in conversation discoveries yet to be made, but demonstrated to all her keenness of intellect.

And then one day, one day when the Way seemed unwilling to come forth. On a day the Way was acting almost like a truculent child, they heard the Raven scream.

John went white. "It's time!" he exclaimed. "You must remember everything I've taught you!" Then he did something Alexi had been dreaming about since she first met him in the bookstore, he pulled her toward him and kissed her on the lips. And then, although she was still in a state of euphoria, he grabbed her hand and started them running back to the manor house. Alexi thought they were all but flying they were moving so quickly. It's when she remembered they had never practiced their leap back in time to the Titanic.

chapter 12

FLEAS

"Run Alexi, run as fast as you can. They're here!" cried John over his shoulder as he dragged her toward not the house but the stables. As they came up out of the gardens they could see and hear the raven circling over the top of at least six coaches all in a row rapidly approaching Woolsthorpe.

As both of them came up to the stables John still holding Alexi by the wrist brought them to a skidding halt in the soft crushed stone. "I need you to go to the back of the house through the kitchen, there's a hall that leads up to the attic. Do you know where that is?" asked John urgently.

Breathing very hard as the run in her eighteenth century garb and clumsy shoes was not easy, Alexi could only nod.

"I need you to be brave. Matthew will've taken care to put all of the servants into suspended animation. I need you to get up to the attic and lock yourself in. Don't use the Way except to escape to where we discussed. If you use the Way for anything but the jump in time they'll find you. Remember, its power leaves a trace, a telltale light. If you do need to go into the past, once you jump back in time you'll be safe. They'll have no idea where you've gone. Do you understand?" asked John.

"John, please don't leave me. I'm not ready," she was nearly in hysterics. "Let me stay by your side it's the only place I feel safe."

"It's too dangerous, you can do this Alexi," said John, who had almost magically calmed his voice and in so doing calmed her. "I'll lead them to the stables. It's all part of the plan."

Despite her fear Alexi couldn't help but mumble, "Well, if it's part of the plan." John smiled, gave her once last hug and pushed her off toward the kitchen.

As Alexi ran toward the back of the house, John turned and calmly walked toward the stables where he saw Matthew beckoning him to hurry. The Raven flying in front of Gottfried's carriages flew directly through the two open doors into the building. As the coaches pulled up to the circular drive the Raven gave them one last yell from inside the stables and then John and Matthew backed in as well leaving the double doors invitingly open.

It didn't take long for Gottfried and all of his men to get out of the coaches and travel the short distance to the stables. The barn was dark the only light coming in through the two open doors. Gottfried and his men entered from the sunlight and it took them a moment to adjust their eyesight. Gottfried, had brought twenty men with him. As they entered the barn they spread out on either side of him.

Gottfried immediately saw John, who was approximately ten feet from the entry. The only figure that Gottfried's men could see clearly. "Well, well the prodigal son returns to his homestead," came the gruff voice. "You picked a pleasant place to die Johnny, sort of full circle. A mathematician would find solace in the Gleichgewicht *(equilibrium)*." He gave a wicked smile and rubbed his gloved hands together. "You left us before we had a chance to finish our tea in New York. We were just getting to the fun part."

John didn't even acknowledge Gottfried's existence as he knew this would enrage him. Rather, he looked toward Matthew, who gave John a quick nod telling him everything was ready. John looked up at the rafters and saw the Raven fly into place, letting out a muted caw.

Gottfried followed John's gaze up to the bird and scowled, "I think I'll stuff that bloody bird," his henchmen laughed in unison as if on cue. They hadn't seen their leader in such a good mood lately. Especially after five of them had been pulled apart by sharks, adding to the substantial losses they had suffered in New York City where John had inexplicably escaped from them. All in all since John's escape Gottfried had lost nearly a third of his followers.

As a group, they were unaccustomed to losing. They had started to consider themselves as immortal and without equal. Many of them had joined Gottfried within the last forty years. Until John's escape, they never believed all the stories Remy and some of Gottfried's older lieutenants had told them about John and Matthew. They thought it was all a fairy tale hyped up trying to make John sound important and in so doing raise Remy's own status in the organization. But now, as twenty of them stood around their leader they were on edge. John Newton had done something they thought impossible, he had led dozens of them directly to their deaths. He had beaten not only Remy, but Gottfried as well. He had broken free of the cursed bookstore something they thought was impossible. Adding to their nervousness was the fact Gottfried had seen it necessary to bring twenty of them to confront, they thought, only John and Matthew.

Once the five survivors of the skirmish, Gottfried had called the Bermuda Triangle, had decoded the papers left by John, supposedly to his lost father Isaac, they knew for certain where to find John. On the ride to Woolsthorpe there had been a great deal of false bravado. They attributed the New York City events as simply them being unprepared. They'd underestimated John and Matthew something they would never do again. This time they were ready. This time they had all made a vow to Gottfried, sealed with their blood, they would all willingly accept disfigurement if they were the one lucky enough to kill either John or Matthew. All of them were ready to get these men behind them and get back to running their world.

Another thing that they accepted, but had grumbled about, Gottfried had forbidden any of them to bring weapons. The sinister side of the Way could be sketchy at times. Having a gun or even a knife was a useful fallback that normally could be enhanced by the shadows. However, Remy told the story as to how he and three other of their comrades had been overtaken in the subway. He noted how during that confrontation John had controlled the owners of the weapons to eliminate their own numbers. From what they were able to piece together, they felt Matthew had used a similar tactic when men left the tea party and went in search of the crow. Here at Woolsthorpe they would rely only on the power available to them from the dark mists of the shadows. Accordingly, Gottfried had brought only those of his followers that were exceedingly strong in the dark way. With the exception of Remy, he brought only his younger followers who held little knowledge of John, Matthew or the light. They had all been screened by Remy to make certain they had no hidden afflictions that John could trigger. He assured all those selected that there was no reason to fear any outcome other than victory. There would be no lack of confidence in this engagement.

Gottfried eyed the stables, swatted away a few of the always present pests and took in the old smell of a time when stables were common place. It brought back old memories, Gottfried spoke again, "This is good Johnny. No one here from the past. Just us to come to terms."

He nodded towards Matthew and continued, "What in the world did you ever hope to accomplish? Surely you knew how futile all this was?" Gottfried waved his hand and his men spread out around the perimeter of the stable, each looking for the best path available to try and kill John. Each hoping they would have a chance to reap the promised riches.

"Where's the trollop Johnny? I promised her to Remy. You haven't sold her off to any slavers have you?" Gottfried smiled evilly trying to provoke John. Yet, Gottfried felt ill at ease something was not feeling quite right. He actually had to fight down the urge to run. It must be the missing girl, he thought, there's something about that girl. "Remy," he called, "go find your girlfriend make sure she's not up to something." All Gottfried's men whistled and jeered as Remy's deformed body limped willingly from the building. Gottfried was happy to sense that this upset John and Matthew, he was right the stupid girl was part of their plan somehow.

A few of the men continued to throw some insults toward the departing Remy, but most were on edge and quieted quickly. They felt it unwise to antagonize John any farther. They feared Gottfried when he was angry, which was most of the time. However, they feared just being in John's presence. All the people in the stables had been at the tea party in New York City and heard what he had done recently in Bermuda."

"You always did talk too much," said a voice from the shadows. It was not Matthew it couldn't possibly be Isaac. He had checked, Isaac was in London playing at the mint. Who then thought Gottfried?

From the stable shadows hidden by their use of the Way emerged a group of five men; Hooke, Wren, Halley, Whiston and Cotes. Despite the peril they had all happily volunteered, it seemed to know Gottfried was to hate Gottfried. They stood behind a table that contained what seemed to be a mad scientist's (Isaac's) chemistry set. It was filled with test tubes, copper tubing and a series of bottles containing every sort of chemical. With a touch put forth by each man in turn a globule of fire was generated in front of them. It gave an eerie light to the darkened stables and lit up each of the men's faces. Wren took a globule of fire to Matthew, Hooke took one to John and Cotes actually climbed up a ladder and placed one in front of where the Raven perched.

"Ah, Hooke, Wren and is that Halley, yes, well how nice I get to see you all again," said Gottfried ignoring Whiston and Cotes. None of them showing up seemed to concern Gottfried whatsoever. "Even if you are only shades. You see Johnny we eliminated each of your father's cohorts as they attempted to rescue you," Gottfried paused. "Yes, you were simply the bait Johnny. It's why I didn't kill you. Or should I say why Remy didn't kill you." Gottfried's men chortled nervously. "Only Matthew was smart enough to avoid elimination. Only, at present, well Matthew your time is up and Johnny it looks like you'll die among your early acquaintants. I think it best not to kill the men behind the table. We don't want to change the present," Gottfried gave these instructions to his troops. "We like the present just the way it is. Right Johnny?" He mocked John once again.

Matthew spoke, "Gottfried, you always were a fool. Everyone at the table slipped into the future. You eliminated no one. They're all waiting for you, including Isaac."

This seemed to take Gottfried, back a step, he really had thought them dead. "Well, no matter, they are eliminated from my present." He spoke with bravura, but he began to sweat a little more.

"Actually," said John as he spoke for the first time. "It's you who are about to be removed Gottfried. You and any man you brought that fails to take this one chance to fall to their knees and repent. We give you and all your men, one last chance. Well, except for Remy, he's already hiding.

So what say you, one last chance to leave this abomination and ask for forgiveness?" John spoke turning to face each man in the circle, knowing no one would leave Gottfried's side but also knowing it was necessary he offer them this opportunity. He did not enjoy seeing men die even those opposed to him and he wanted no retribution from the Way.

Gottfried though sweating and finding it necessary to swat away a couple more fleas said, "Really, Johnny there are twenty of us and but seven of you. Not counting that flea bitten krähe (*crow*)." As he said this Gottfried swatted a flea from his ear that had drawn blood. These things are more vicious than I remember he thought as he gave a slight smile to see several of his men also having a problem with the fleas. Oh, the joys of the seventeenth century, he thought. John and his companions did not seem to have the same problem as the lights they each held seemed to keep the insects at bay.

"Let's get this over with," said one of his lieutenants. "This filthy place is crawling with vermin, it's infested," as he to swat at an unseen pest.

At this the Raven let out a cry. "Yes," said Hooke never one to let the conversation go unaided. "I think we can confirm all of the huntsmen have been bitten John. As the man said, this place is crawling with vermin. Let's get this over with."

Gottfried turned on the spot to stare away from John and toward Hooke. "Was fur ein spiel ist das? (*What game is this?*)"

"Ah well, Gottfried you were on the mainland in 66 when all the fuss broke out," piped in Wren. "Oh, for you not yet born that's 1666 and the outbreak was the bubonic plague. I tell you it was nasty stuff gentlemen."

It was as if an explosion had taken place, Gottfried's loyal followers faces turned immediately from confidence to terror as they looked for an explanation from their general.

Halley picked up the line of conversation, "the plague actually stayed with us for many years. Even this year, thirty-four years later saw an outbreak. However, the vaccine Isaac and John brought back here to Woolsthorpe kept us and all the staff healthy. Alas, not so all the fleas."

"Well," chuckled Matthew, "it kept everyone at Woolsthorpe healthy up to now." He moved the globule of light around in the air in front of him. "Even after having had the vaccine, these fleas are annoying. Of course, these lights keep the wee buggers away. Ye and all your men will know the bubonic plague is transmitted by flea bites, right Gottfried?"

Gottfried began to comprehend and he chortled, "You think by merely infecting us with the plague you'll be able to put off your deaths. The pest (*black plague*) takes hours to strike. You'll be dead and we'll be back in New York in time to grab an antidote." Despite this strident summary Gottfried's followers looked shocked. Several started to react violently to the many bites they were taking. Once a flea draws blood the rest of his companions attack even more voraciously.

"You were right John," said Whiston softly. "There appear to be no takers among them. No one fears the Lord in this group." And with this pronouncement, it was Whiston that had given the signal. It was time. John started it all in motion with a nod toward the Raven. The Raven swooped down at Gottfried and as the Raven drew everyone's attention, the seven men dropped their pods of fire on the straw. They also put opaque glasses that Hooke and John had manufactured days ago around their heads. The pods alit in the straw rather than generating fire produced a thick smoke which rolled on the floor of the stables. The thick fog it produced would make it more difficult for Gottfried and his men to call the shadows.

As the bird flew at Gottfried, both let out screams of rage. The Raven didn't wait around for Gottfried's reaction, he flew to his enemy's face, then quickly flew out the stable doors which were magically closing at the Raven's direction. John didn't want to risk injury to the Raven's eyes.

While all this was taking place, Gottfried's men tried to pull on the strength of the shadows and direct it at the seven men facing them. Gottfried had turned his rage, and hence his portion of the shadows at the fleeing bird. It was for this reason, his head turned toward the door and not facing the seven men opposing him, that his eyes were not as ruined as those of his troops.

As Gottfried and his men all concentrated on pulling up the shadows, John and his friends, with opaque glasses at the ready pulled up the brightest light from the Way each could find. It was as if the light and the energy of the sun had been released seven times over into the once darkened room. Once they called the light they slipped behind their leaden goggles.

The seven allies were protected by the lead glasses. Of course, neither Gottfried nor any of his men were protected. To make matters worse for them they had all been focused on pulling up the shadows despite the fog rolling on the floor of the stables. This required the iris in their eyes to greatly narrow as they searched for the gray light in the dark stables. As such, when the blinding light was released in the stables their eyes were wide open. The bright light of the Way burst through their pupils and seared their retinas. They were all immediately blinded. They would no longer be able to call the shadows and they were all infected with bubonic plague from multiple flea bites.

When he was satisfied that the light had faded. John removed his leaden goggles and seeing that everything had gone according to plan gave a shout of all clear. All his friends saw what he now saw, twenty blind men writhing in pain rolling on the floor or trying to wave off the never ending flea bites. It gave neither John nor his friends any feeling of joy or victory. As he began to step over the bodies of his enemies, he announced, "The stables will be sealed Gottfried. You and your misguided men will all perish by morning. I suggest you take that time and pray for forgiveness."

As John opened the door and all his friends left. He heard Gottfried screaming in rage and pain yell, "Sie haben noch nicht Johnny gewonnen. Ich habe immer noch das Madcgen. (*You haven't won yet Johnny. I still have the girl.*)"

A shiver went up John's spine and he sprang out the door at a run. Half flying, half gliding toward the manor house's attic. All his friends knew of the danger to Alexi and they ran after him, not sure what they'd find but they all feared the worst.

chapter 13

THE SHADOWS

Alexi rushed into the house torn between cowering in the attic as John had instructed her and standing beside him as he faced Gottfried. She realized how pathetic her powers were compared to everyone else but she was not sure she could manage being alone, being without John or Matthew to protect her. If only the Raven would have accompanied her she would have felt less afraid. By the time she reached the attic door at the foot of the stairs, she was shaking almost uncontrollably. At first she thought the door to the attic might be locked, but a third try at the seventeenth century latch gave her access to a dark damp stairwell. She looked around and was able to see a candle on a kitchen counter and getting it lit from the kitchen fire provided her enough light to enable her to make her way up the stairs after locking the door behind her.

When she reached the top of the stairs, she used the candlelight to peer at her surroundings. The room was very large and unlike some house attics, she had seen in her youth, the floor was complete and solid. However, similar to all attics this seventeenth century attic was used for storage. There was old furniture, arms of various nature, lots and lots of swords, even a full suite of rusted and dented armor. The rafters that held up the roof seemed to have no rhyme or reason as it was obvious the house had undergone numerous expansions. She cautiously walked around the rafters until at last she found an old chair. She threw back a sheet that was used as a cover and sat down. Typical, she thought as she sat down and the seat gave way to even her modest weight with a crack.

It was then she realized she had made her first significant mistake. She had only brought up one candle from the kitchen and it was running rather low. If she put it out to save the candle she wouldn't have the means to relight it unless she went back down the stairs to the kitchen. She would never be able to wind her way through the rafters and the stored items without light. She remembered the green ball John had produced for her that first evening on the *Principia* and she felt she could manufacture one with the aid of the Way, but John had warned her not to use the Way, it would leave a trace. However, as she was about to reach a decision, something along the lines of sneaking back to the kitchen, her candle flickered and died away. She was now left in total darkness.

So typical, she thought with a hint of a wry smile, John and Matthew's plans usually stop before my safety comes into consideration. She tried to keep herself calm and not become some ridiculous panic stricken teenager. Besides, she thought, where was her faith in John? She hadn't known John and Matthew long, but she saw what they were capable of doing. Surely when you add such men as Hooke, Wren and Halley, not to mention Whiston and Cotes, well, surely you could defeat any number of Gottfried's men. She had no reason to fear she assured herself. Why she doubted Gottfried would even bring a deformed hunchback like Remy on such a mission. Surely not back to a time when the superstitious people of this age would associate him with the devil. Just thinking of Remy made tears start to well in her eyes and her bravado began to falter. Gottfried's men just couldn't defeat John she thought to herself stubbornly.

Yet, a faint voice in her mind suggested they had defeated him and all his friends. They had entombed John for forty years and at this thought her tears started to fall. She had to admit she was scared. She was not some super heroine. She was just a teenager from West Virginia. Suddenly, she jumped and let out a small shriek at a sound to her right. Was it a rat, a bat? What else was in this room? She would sooner die than fall into Remy's hands again.

It was at this point Alexi made her second mistake, her courage all but gone with no light available sitting in an ancient attic, she called upon the Way and plucking the lime colored light from the many surrounding her she made a small ball of light. It calmed her immediately, it gave her light and it made her realize that John had not left her defenseless. He had taught her to use the Way and he told her where to go if the she needed to escape. If only they had found the time to let her practice jumping through time she would go there now. She was able to dry her eyes and, with the aid of the green ball of light wander farther back into the attic's depths.

Unfortunately for Alexi, the use of the colors of the Way is not meant to be hidden. Unlike the shadows, its purpose is to be proudly displayed and enjoyed by all. With the conceptualization of the little green ball of light a beacon was sent out telling Remy his prize was hidden in amongst the rafters. But how to get up there, where was the attic door in this damn maze of a house?

It wasn't very long after she had pulled the light from the Way that Alexi heard the latch to the attic door open. She immediately realized her mistake and swallowing a scream extinguished her light. All was quiet for a moment and then she heard a small female voice in German say, "This is the only way up to the attic Herr Remy, I agree it's almost impossible to find."

"Danka," said Remy. "Now go and tell Herr Gottfried in the stables that I found the girl that she's only been hiding. I'll only be a few minutes."

The German maid who had braided Alexi's hair that very morning and had pretended to be interested in her wellbeing squealed with laughter. The next thing Alexi could hear was Remy limping up the wooden staircase. She could smell him across the width and breadth of the attic despite all the mold and dampness that otherwise hung in the air.

She was scared, of course, but more than that she was shocked to see how Remy made use of the Way. Rather than the colorful bouncy, almost alive lights of the Way John had introduced to her, Remy's use produced a dark purple mist that oozed across the floor. The purple slime was meant to find her and it wasted little time highlighting her features as she tried to hide behind some stout rafters.

"Did'ja miss me darl'n?" Remy hissed as he reached the last stair. His purple mist had not only highlighted her figure at the back of the attic it lit up his prospective path around the maze of articles strewn across the floor.

He smelled worse and looked even more disfigured from the short time since Alexi had last seen him. As the figure limped closer to her, she noticed that the disfigured man had become even more grotesque. He must have been on a killing spree she thought or perhaps once you misuse the Way the disfigurement never stops. Despite her fear of him, her response was more out of shock at what she saw than some remnant of courage, "You're even more mutated than the last time I saw you."

Remy was at first taken aback by the insult. He expected her to be a wailing wreck. No man or woman had ever dismissed him in such a fashion. Especially one that had survived a first encounter with him. He had punished many of Gottfried's men this past week as many of them had failed to perform properly at the café. His penalty for this misuse of the Way was indeed taking its toll. However, he'd gladly take whatever punishment the Way had in store for him after he dealt with the girl. She would not be taunting him for long. She would be begging. At last they would be rid of Matthew and John. At last he could enjoy the fruits of centuries of hard labor and devotion to his master for which his body had paid such a terrible price. He would have all the time in the world to feast on the girl.

Alexi, drew a sword from its scabbard and pointed it at Remy. It was a rather sturdy blade about three feet in length. She found it was one of the few blades in the attic, she could actually lift.

Remy gave her a look of mock horror that made his disfigured face look, if possible, even more grotesque. "Play'n hard to get are ye. Oh, well, since you've a sword I might as well run along," he mocked Alexi as he limped closer. As he said this he swung his arm and the sword was flung out of her hand and embedded in the beam above her head. He then swept his other arm and the purple slime that had found her caught her by surprise and threw her against one wooden beam and then another. Each time as she absorbed a viscous blow to her body, she found just enough time to protect her head. She let out a screech of pain as the final impact knocked the air from her lungs.

As he made his final approach and stood over her crumpled and now bruised and bloody body, she scuttled away from him as best she could. She felt sure he had cracked her ribs, he might also have a broken her right arm and wrist. She almost blacked out from the pain. He was too strong. His use of the shadow's purple slime to throw her like a ragdoll amongst the rafters had caught her by surprise. Now it heavily clung to her body and held her firmly in place. It felt cold and unforgiving as it coiled around her body. Remy bent down and tore off the sleeve of her gown. She gasped in pain as the sleeve pulled on her broken wrist. With both of his knees pinning her to the ground, he grabbed a small pouch from his coat and from it he pulled out a syringe and a vial of heroine. He had been planning and looking forward to this moment ever since she had fled the café in New York City. "Now, as I remember you become much more respectful with a bit of this in your veins."

chapter 14

GOLD

John, Matthew, Hooke, Wren and Halley all rushed from the stables toward the kitchen. Whiston and Cotes began to follow, but John yelled at them to see to the stable doors and lock everyone inside.

When they came upon the unlocked attic door in the kitchen John anticipated the worst. He ran up the stairs three at a time calling Alexi's name following a bright white light that he called upon from the Way to guide him. He felt terrible that he had not given better thought to Alexi's safety, but he never imagined Gottfried would give her any consideration. As the light penetrated the darkness and lit up the huge room they were overcome with what they saw in the back of the attic.

There on his knees with a syringe in his hand, knelt a solid gold statue of the former Remy Stoltz. The man that had terrorized thousands of men and women over hundreds of years, so deformed from his misuse of the Way that his humanity was barely recognizable.

John knelt by the gold statue and called out, "Alexi, Alexi, you can come out it's over. We won, it's us."

The other men all called out as well, but there was no response. Hooke knelt with John beside the deformed creature not believing what a grotesque beast the man had become, "If there is any plainer statement about the penalty for misuse of the Way," stated Hooke.

"Where is she John?" asked Matthew.

John smiled, "She learns fast, I think I know where I can find her." The other men looked around. "Not here, not this century," added John.

Everyone in the room seemed to relax at John's comment. They were all aware John had been instructing Alexi in the use of the Way and that if she had jumped in time she would be safe. Once at ease and kneeling beside John, Hooke still inspecting the deformed golden creature said, tentatively, "John, if she killed or intended to kill Remy." He paused, his inspection had not convinced him the gargoyle was dead. "Well, I mean even one as vile as him and given from all evidence his malicious intent at the time of his, well, encasement..." it seemed Hooke did not want to say or could not find the delicate words to say what he feared.

"Well, what I mean is," said Hooke with one final try.

"What he means," piped in Wren, "She may have to pay a price John." Wren came over and put a hand on John's shoulder, speaking softly, "It's obvious she used the Way to turn this creature into solid gold."

"Not a metal I would have picked for him," said Matthew.

John looked around for clues as to what may have occurred. Clearly there had been a scuffle. He inspected the statue more closely and then looked up at the rafters, and then let out a slight grin.

"What do you see John?" asked Matthew in a worried voice. He hated to think of one as beautiful as Alexi suffering a penalty when it appeared she had no choice except to use the Way to challenge or kill her attacker.

"It's hard to see, but there's a glancing wound to Remy's shoulder probably from that sword," said John nodding toward a rusty and bloody sword laying off to the side of the statute. John looked up at the rafters above where Alexi must have lain at that last moment, "It appears that sword was wedged in the beam." He said pointing to a place in a ceiling beam that had been recently cut. "Alexi must have dragged herself underneath it and when Remy wasn't looking used the Way to force the blade to drop on him. That would account for that gash on his back and the blood on the blade. Remy would have had no need for a sword."

Hooke nodded in agreement, "I agree John, but a falling blade from that short a distance would have only given him a glancing blow, it probably enraged him more than harmed him. So that's when she reached out for the Way and delivered the blackguard some justice. Still, if for instance, he threw the blade into the beam, which seems likely, and then she tried to dissuade him with its use then perhaps her penalty will be slight."

"I hope that's how it happened. She's such a delightful and beautiful child," said Wren, "I do hope she's not punished for what she had to do."

"You know John, you really must explain this injection device to me before you go," added Halley looking at the needle that had turned to gold in Remy's hand. Such a device would not be seen for another hundred and fifty years.

"Another time Halley," said John a bit exasperated at the timing of the question. "While I don't think she'll be in any immediate danger. I should go to her, she'll be scared and frightened."

"What's to be done back at the stables John?" asked Matthew.

"Yes, we need to get back there," said Halley. At this all the men turned their back on Remy the Gold and hurried back down the attic stairs.

As they emerged from the kitchen they could hear what sounded like Cotes calling for help. All the men broke into a run toward the stables. When they arrived back at the stables they found Cotes huddled over an unconscious Whiston. The stable doors had been closed and barred.

"Cotes, what happened?" asked Matthew running to his side beside the wounded Whiston. Matthew immediately called upon the Way and pulled a lavender light to hover over Whiston.

As Whiston regained consciousness a relieved Cotes explained, "It was that German maid, Bertha or whatever her name is. I was reconnoitering the perimeter of the stables while Whiston guarded the front doors. We had barred them of course. All the men inside were screaming and banging into one another and the doors. It sounded like complete chaos inside. We heard Gottfried yelling at everyone to remain calm, but no one was paying him any attention. When I came back around to the front I saw Whiston here knocked out with that bloody gash in his head and I saw that girl helping Gottfried into the first carriage. I ran and reclosed the doors so no one else could escape and by the time I did that the carriage had taken off. That's when I called for help and came over to attend to Whiston. I'm sorry John it all happened so quickly."

John realized Cotes was deeply upset by what had happened on his watch. He patted Cotes on the shoulder, "It's not your fault Cotes. We all rushed off to look after Alexi, we should have left you more help to look after so many prisoners."

"How's Alexi?" were the first words spoken by an awakening Whiston.

John smiled at Whiston's show of concern despite the serious wound he had suffered, "I imagine she's in better shape than you are right now, but perhaps a bit more scared." John reached out his hand and helped Whiston to his feet. "How do you feel?" asked John.

"A bit shaky," stammered Whiston. "I only caught a glimpse of the girl that hit me. Did she get anyone out of the stables?"

"I think only Gottfried," said Hooke returning to his comrades after inspecting the group of men still yelling and banging at the stable doors. Hooke had used the Way to slip a green light under the doors and project back to himself an accurate picture of what was happening behind the closed doors.

"They'll be settling down pretty quickly that strain is particularly virulent. They won't survive the morning," said Wren.

They were all disappointed that Gottfried had escaped. Still, they had wiped out over half of his men and Alexi had deprived Gottfried of Remy's services. It had all been accomplished with only the cut and concussion suffered by Whiston. Perhaps, most importantly, it had been accomplished in a vacuum. The only loose end may be the German maid.

The men moved away from the stables from which the shouts of desperation could still be heard. "The German maid," said Matthew, "that's what Gottfried meant, when he said he still had the girl. He wasn't referring to Alexi at all. I thought the light I pulled from the Way would have captured everyone in suspension, I don't know how she escaped. I thought I checked on her and she was out."

"She must have protected herself somehow or she has some inkling of how to use the shadows. She's been underfoot all this time," said Halley.

"Funny thing is I never remembered her even being here. She must have been…" as John spoke it dawned on him. "She must have been a plant, she must be from the future planted here by Gottfried before his men arrived." He turned to his friends, "Do any of you remember her? Matthew, did you ever see her in the future with Gottfried in New York?"

"I'm not certain John, we was usually run'n for our lives," Matthew said with his brows furrowed. "Gottfried usually used men." he tugged at his beard. "I may have seen her in the bookstore, best ask the Raven."

"Why does this matter so much," asked Cotes. "Shouldn't we be after Gottfried?"

"Yes, we should," said John, "but unless she's from the future than the past may be changed. She won't be here to live out her miserable life and our access, as well as Gottfried's, to the present will vanish."

The Raven came flying over to John's shoulder. No words passed John's lips, but after a few moments the Raven left out a long caw and flew in the direction of Gottfried's fleeing carriage.

"Did he remember seeing her John?" asked Matthew.

"Yes, he's certain that she was the one that kicked him from the window the night Alexi and I first met. Our ability to get back to the present shouldn't be in danger." John sighed in relief.

"Aye, but it will include Gottfried unless we can catch him," said Matthew.

"He's wounded and we've inflicted a heavy blow to his organization. It's even more important that we make sure these men die, at this place in time. If Gottfried thinks of a way to save them or God forbid, they get out and spread the plague, well, either way the ramifications could be disastrous."

John thinking rapidly said, "I suspect Gottfried and the maid will flee back to New York City as soon as possible. He'll need medical attention for the plague as well as his eyes. Bertha may contract the plague as well. Gottfried was infested with fleas. I'm sure there's no use going after him at this point. I have to go after Alexi. I need the rest of you to see things through here. See to their deaths and their burial. Get rid of those horses and coaches in the yard before you bring the rest of the staff out of suspension. Explain to them Alexi and I went to see Isaac in London." They all nodded in response. The fact that they could use the Way in helping to bury Gottfried's men made the task seem less onerous.

"I don't know how to thank each and every one of you," said John solemnly. "In the future, you all came for me. You all give up your time in the present to free me against impossible odds. I don't know how I can ever repay you."

They all smiled and Wren spoke for all of them when he said, "We'll always be here for you John."

"John, when this thing is all settled with Gottfried, you and Matthew come back and visit with us," said Halley.

"Aye," said Cotes, "and bring Miss Alexi."

They all laughed in agreement.

"What I want to know," said Hooke, "is how Matthew saved you while the rest of us had to slip into the future."

"I'll let Matthew fill you in," declared John, "it's an amazing story best told before the staff is woken." John hugged each man in turn, Hooke, Halley, Wren, Whiston and Cotes. Eventually, he turned to Matthew and said, "I'll see you back in New York, at the café."

As John made to leave Matthew grabbed his arm, "John, I suspect I know where you told Alexi to go. If it's the Titanic, it's not safe. Let me go with you," said Matthew.

"No, Matthew you're needed here to set these deaths in time," responded John nodding to the stables.

"At least take the Raven with ye, someone to watch your back," said Matthew.

"Yes," said John thoughtfully, "that may be best. I suspect Gottfried had a lot of his men on the docks in those days. I'll ask the Raven to join me." As he went to pull away Matthew drew him into a bear hug.

John looked a bit bewildered at the emotion nodded one time and said "See you in New York." At that he summoned the blue-gray light of the Way, turned and disappeared.

After John disappeared Matthew said, looking at the light, "be careful John." Matthew, who knew John best of all was worried that he was seeing John for the last time. He was concerned that if John saw Alexandra looking out over the railing of the deck of the Titanic he would never come back to their present. He would stay with Alexandra get off the boat in Cherbourg, where he knew it had stopped before heading out to the Atlantic, and they would be lost together in time forever.

chapter 15

THE WAY'S FAVORITE

Alexi spun out of the blue light into an alley near a busy pier. Her trip had not been easy. It was as if she were fighting a fierce storm blowing into her face the whole way. Events in time seemed to rush by on either side of her as she edged forward. However, she was so relieved to be out of the attic that she envisioned the fierce wind rushing by her as cleansing her from what she had just endured.

If she had a calendar and a watch she could have observed it was near noon on April 10, 1912. She stood looking out at what was the pier of her dreams. She would have thought calling it her nightmare, but after what she had just endured, it was all in all rather tame. The events she had just lived through, now those are what nightmares are made of she assured herself. At least I survived in one piece she thought. Or had she, she still felt the ringing in her ears of her screams mixed together with Remy's as his body hardened inch by inch into pure gold. His retched smell as he had pursued and captured her still filled her nostrils. She looked down and saw a trickle of blood running down her arm from where the needle had scratched her as she wiggled out from under the heavy golden statue. She tried to gather a deep breath only to be reminded that her ribs were probably broken. Her breathing was labored as she limped away from a crowd further back into the alley trying to get her bearings. She held her right arm close to her chest with her left hand. Her right arm and wrist were throbbing. She was in a great deal of pain.

It took all her effort not to scream and vomit where she stood. When Remy had thrown her against the wall the last time she had been able to crawl and position herself underneath the sword dangling in the attic rafter. The only light available was being emitted from the horrid, acrid, vile purple slime. Ironically, it was the sight of the syringe full of heroin that gave her the courage she needed. She was able to focus and call on the Way to release the sword. The blade only glanced off Remy's shoulder and while it was not enough to kill him it was enough to distract him. The blade had pierced an old wound of Remy's, one the Way refused to let heal. Remy screamed in pain and his screams emboldened Alexi further who realized she no longer had to fear her tormentor. With the blood from his opened wound dripping onto her face Alexi called upon the Way once again. She used the last of her strength, her sanity, to call upon the one light that stood out to her among all others, the golden light. She directed it to embrace the hideous monster. She realized now she could have called upon the blue-gray light to escape and leave Remy alive, but she had chosen the gold. She also realized now she should expect to be punished. Especially since when Remy's final scream was frozen in gold she felt victorious and not a trace of remorse.

At that point, she had no idea what was happening in the stables. She had no idea if John, Matthew or any of his friends were alive. All she knew was she had to run, she had to flee Woolsthorpe and seek safety in a place only John could find her. She crawled out from under the golden statue and conjured up the blue-gray light of the Way. She spun on the spot with only the vision of her dream etched in her DNA to guide her. The fact that she discovered herself at the pier didn't surprise her. As she spun, she knew she would make it. What did surprise her was that she seemed not to have been punished for her misuse of the Way. Perhaps, she hoped, the broken wrist, arm and ribs were sufficient retribution. She remembered when Remy had killed that man in New York City he was immediately malformed. Maybe, she thought, the disfigurement from using the Way to kill or maim someone takes a bit more time to materialize if it's your first incident.

She still had on her early eighteenth century garb and this was now the early twentieth century. The fact she was spotted with blood and looked half crazed made her realize why she was attracting so many stares even in the sparsely populated alley. She quickly ducked behind a truck with a canvas trailer and still fearing she might slip into unconsciousness from the pain at last called upon the lavender mist of the Way. The relief was almost instantaneous as her rib cage seemed to heal and her breathing became unimpaired. Her arm and wrist seemed to snap back into place. The lavender hue offered the added benefit of seeming to lift her spirits and calm her nerves. If she was to be penalized, she thought at least the Way didn't hesitate to come to her aide. She decided she would have to remember the lavender light's calming effect as she could have used it every day since she met John. Before she left the alley, she pulled the red light of the Way and as she had seen John do before she was able to change her clothes. Once again, she was replacing blood stained clothes. When will this nightmare end she asked herself.

All in all, as she strolled back out to watch the hustle and bustle of everyone preparing themselves for the voyage, she felt surprisingly calm and a bit proud of herself. She had managed to use and direct the Way to her benefit independent of John's or Matthew's instructions. She had escaped the nightmare that was Remy. However, her fear of what retribution she would suffer from her misuse of the Way in her escape put a pale over her exuberance.

As she walked back to watch the ship, she was surprised at how familiar it all looked to her. Everything was as it had appeared in her dreams. Except, she realized, in her dreams she was on the deck of the Titanic looking out. She quickly moved to a position that would enable her to see the spot on the deck which in her dreams she had looked out from onto the traffic laden pier with such longing and heaviness of heart. Alexi's hands came up to her mouth in shock at her first sight of Alexandra standing there alone on the second deck. She was without a doubt the most beautiful woman she had ever seen. Was there any conceivable way she could ever emanate such grace or beauty? Amazingly, as she watched from behind a pillar she noted a ship's crew member introduce himself to Alexandra. From her dreams, she knew exactly what the captain, Edwin Smith, would be saying. He would be inviting her to his table for dinner that evening. It was at this introduction, near noon that the ship began the release of the ropes tying it to the world of the living to be pulled by tug out of the Southampton harbor. It was on its way to Cherbourg, France and from there to Queenstown, Ireland and then at last to its destiny.

"She was very beautiful. You couldn't walk down a city street in London without carriages coming to a halt," said a sad voice beside her. "She was the Way's favorite," he hungrily gazed at Alexandra, who was still looking out over the railing, looking for him.

Alexi's body eased at just the sound of his voice. She wanted to throw her arms around his neck and kiss him with all her might. In a rush she turned and saw the longing in his eyes. Her thought at that moment was she wished that someday someone might love her as much as John loved Alexandra. The moment lost she hesitated and said, "I'm sorry, the Way's favorite?"

"What," asked John now far off with his thoughts? He was so relieved to find Alexi apparently unharmed that he left his mind drift off in his own sea of thoughts.

"You said the Way's favorite," prodded Alexi.

John smiled weakly perhaps for all that had been lost. "It was an amazing phenomenon, she attracted the light of the Way without even calling for it. The longer she knew of it, became intimate with its beauty, the more it endowed her with its own beauty. She could charm a raven from its tail feather," John chuckled.

"Sorry," said Alexi once again. She had never heard John speak of Alexandra before. She couldn't even remember him, offering up much about his past unless she was quizzing him.

"Alexandra would have long conversations with the Raven. Mostly they would talk about the beauty of flying. Of course, with the Way, Alexandra could fly, but she wanted to know what the Raven saw with his incredible eyesight? How he felt with the wind carrying him in its embrace. She told me on several occasions she dreamed she was flying with or as the Raven. She could see the earth below her as the Raven saw it. I can speak to the Raven, but not on the level of intimacy she achieved. He would even bring her his tail feather, his most prized possession."

"Yes," said Alexi excitedly, "I've had those dreams. I've accepted his tail feather before."

John looked at her bemused, "The Way is more than magic tricks. It's alive and to those of whom it chooses to reveal itself, it builds a beautiful everlasting relationship. It simply adored Alexandra."

"We have to save her," cried Alexi. "We have to get her off that ship." She turned to beg John to act, to use the Way to save Alexandra.

"There is no means possible," said John sadly. "Our present would be changed."

"But that would be a good thing," cried Alexi. "The future from here holds two world wars and millions will be killed. We could save her, the ship and change everything."

"Time doesn't work that way Alexi. I've told you we'd merely set out on a new path, a new braid, from this moment forward. The current course of history, our present, would go on without us. Besides, how do you know we would win again?" said John softly.

"But," Alexi looked at John, who was fighting back the tears as he gazed at his wife, his love, sailing towards her tragic destiny.

"You could save her John. You can do anything!" exclaimed Alexi.

"I can't change the laws of nature and physics. There is no way Alexi," said John in an emotionally strained voice. "To even attempt such a thing would be inviting catastrophe, everything would be put at risk. Once started there is no going back."

It was at this stage in the conversation that the Raven came flying down to land on John's shoulder. The bird winked at Alexi, softly cawed and then flew off once again to catch one last glimpse of his and the Way's favorite.

"The Raven says there are five of Gottfried's men aboard that ship. We'd have had no chance to even visit her. This was all set up as a trap to capture me. When I failed to show they decided that their best option was to kill Alexandra and in so doing destroy me. I've never allowed myself to come to this place. I was afraid I'd never be strong enough to leave. It seems she was waiting for me till the end," he paused gathering his strength. "I was away tending to other desperate matters. Unfortunately, I never found a light that allowed me to be in two places at one time," a tear finally slipped from his eye.

"I'm so sorry," was all Alexi could think to say the tears began to slip down her face.

Her tears brought John out of his reverie. He took Alexi's hand and spun her on the spot. His voice lightened as he cleared his throat and focused on matters at hand. "Other than the retched new clothes I see you wearing. I see no other punishment or ill effects from the mischief you served to our murderous Remy."

"Is he dead?" She asked, coming back to her own dilemma.

"If not, he's providing an excellent representation," said John.

"I tried to use gravity to get a sword that he threw to drop on him, make his death his own fault like you instructed me. The blade, however, only gave him a glancing blow and it only made him more furious. He was too strong for me John, it was risk disfigurement, or death," tears now streamed down her face full force. "I realize now I should have just used the Way to come here, but the only light the Way seemed to show me at that moment was gold."

Suddenly, John frowned and rubbed the side of Alexis' face just above her lips. "Well," said John, "it will require some getting used to."

"What?" she asked her tears slowing. She wiped her face with the back of her sleeve where John had just touched her.

"It seems," said John producing a mirror out of thin air and handing it to her, "that the Spirit has settled on the punishment you shall have to bear henceforth for your crime."

Alexi grabbed the mirror in shock, "Oh, no," she rubbed at her new mole. "Can you get rid of it John?"

John chuckled, "Alas, my lady there is nothing I can do. I suspect the Spirit has taken into consideration the necessity of your act and the nature of your victim and has left you a small reminder."

"A small reminder?" squeaked Alexi still staring at the mirror and rubbing at her new birth mark.

"Yes," said John, "if you call upon the Way there are consequences for any misuse."

Alexi nodded, handing John back the mirror, then asked, "And your plan. Did you kill Gottfried and his men? Are we safe?"

John had almost forgotten, almost, "Gottfried is like a cockroach, it seems the chamber maid Bertha may have been a plant from the future. When we rushed to see to your well-being, she helped him escape."

"I'm sorry," she said.

"It's not your fault. We should have been better prepared," said John. "He came upon us much faster than I anticipated. I thought he'd be more cautious and we'd have a bit more time. Perhaps his plant, Bertha, gave him the encouragement to attack quickly. Bertha may have told him that I was instructing you in the use of the Way which is why he sent Remy to account for you. I'm sorry we had to keep you in the dark about our plans, but there was so much at risk we couldn't rule out the possibility you might be captured or kidnapped. Come to think of it, I'm surprised Bertha didn't drag you off to Gottfried."

"Is that why you spent so much time with me, to protect me?" Alexi was not sure she wanted to hear the answer. Was John only spending time with her because he felt he needed to be with her so his plan wouldn't be jeopardized?

"Alexi, my time with you… well, there's no place I'd rather be," said John.

Alexi wasn't sure what her relationship with John was meant to be. For her part she found herself falling in love with him. But, perhaps that was only Alexandra's memories. She saw how he had looked upon her just now as the boat had slipped away. John would always love her, how do you fight a memory Alexi asked herself. Suddenly, the dock seemed to swirl up around her, she started to spin to lose consciousness when John caught her and folded her into his arms.

"Are you OK?" he asked with obvious concern.

"I'm fine, just… too much blood… too many emotions," she said. "This is almost too much for a girl from the foothills of West Virginia." She had blanched and felt a strange chill come over her.

John half carried, half led her to a place to sit down. He pulled the lavender mist around her and she breathed a sigh of relief.

It took her a few minutes for her heart to calm down, to feel the life being pumped back through her body. Perhaps it's best just to focus on things at hand, she said to herself. She took a deep breath and smiled weakly, "I always thought something was strange about her. I never trusted her from the first time Matthew led me to my room the first night at Woolsthorpe. I could never figure out what it was. I can tell you she was deathly afraid of the Raven," said Alexi.

It took John a minute to realize Alexi was talking about Bertha. John realized Alexi must have been overcome by a moment of shock from all that she had just been through. The kid could only be so tough said John to himself. He gave Alexi a hug and out of thin air pulled her a pewter mug of hot tea which she gladly accepted.

"Yes, it all fits. The Raven would have exposed her if he had seen her. In any case, she and Gottfried are both on the run and her master is terribly wounded," said John.

"And the others, is Matthew safe?" asked Alexi trying to focus on things that really mattered.

"Yes, Whiston caught a nasty blow to the head, but the Way healed him. They all wanted to come, but they have to see after the death of nineteen of Gottfried's associates. We used the force of the Way to blind them and fleas to infect them with the plague. Blinded they can't call upon the Way or in their case the shadows. They'll all pay for their sins," said John solemnly.

Finally, after Alexi had finished her tea, they began to walk arm in arm away from the pier away from the past. The Raven had flown back, signaling the all clear from above. John heaved a sigh of relief.

Alexi asked, "John, if Bertha was sent to uncover your plan and she knew all your friends were there to help. Why did Gottfried still attack?"

"The shadows are the dark underbelly of the Way. When one such as Gottfried calls up the shadows, it's like a thick sludge that blocks every access to the light. Remember what they did in the bookstore? That was probably just two or three of them. Here he brought twenty men with him. He teaches his apprentices to do nothing more than invoke this darkness. He knew Matthew and I would have all of our friends, however, he felt he had more than enough men to block out the light. Fortunately, he was wrong. We never gave them a chance to pull upon the shadows, we acted quickly to blind them and then they were without the means to call their bloody shadows. Gottfried must have prevented them from bringing arms as he thought we would use the weapons against them. However, that was never our plan. We never knew how many he would bring or how they might be armed. We knew the fleas could bite as many men as he dared to bring and that there was no means of him being able to kill all the fleas. Our plan allowed us to infect as many of Gottfried's men as he brought with him. The only trick was to make sure we got them all into the stables."

Alexi, thought a moment, "John, how were we ever able to escape from New York then? There must have been fifty men surrounding us?"

John smiled, "Surprise. Over confidence and then at some point panic and fear. If you remember they couldn't see Matthew. They only heard the Raven and saw their comrades falling one by one. Their growing fear, despite Gottfried's bravado, prevented them from blocking my access to the light."

"And you," said Alexi looking up into John's face as they continued to walk arm in arm from the pier back to the alley.

"Pardon," responded John stopping to look down into her emerald eyes.

"You." said Alexi, "Your bravery John. Your power."

"Perhaps," said John. He drew her close, "Are you alright?"

Alexi nodded, "except for the mole."

They both smiled weakly. John turned and took one last look at the horizon. The tug boat was taking the Titanic out to her destiny. John caught a glimpse of the sunlight reflecting off the four smoke stacks and said, "After Isaac slipped into the future, he has only been able to communicate with me one time. It was a message I uncovered on a desk at Woolsthorpe on November 12, 1918 the day after the First World War ended. I can only imagine he left it there reaching back into the past, hoping I would find it on that day. It said simply that he and my mother were very proud of me."

Alexi looked at John gazing out at the departing ship in shock at what she heard, "But you said your mother died at your birth?"

"Yes," said John responding slowly. "He wanted me to know that the future, however, distant allows loved ones to be reunited. And despite my loss of Alexandra I had a task laid upon me at birth to protect the present."

Alexi after all she had been through had a tough time trying to understand the implications from what John told her. All she could think to do was embrace him and kiss his cheek as John still stared after the ship.

After the Titanic slid out of view John turned to Alexi and said softly, "Her specialty seemed to be the lavenders and softer hues of the Way. She could heal almost any illness given time. She would walk into a field hospital after a battle and pain would all but jump from her presence. I've seen her ease many a dying man's pain as he passed to the other side, she was special, not strong in all aspects of the Way, but in the gentler softer colors. But," he said as he looked into Alexi's emerald eyes, "Alexandra didn't have your strength or amazing courage."

chapter 16

THE PRESENT

The free fall through time seemed a bit tougher this time. Alexi concluded that going back in time felt like jumping off a cliff while going forward felt like sailing into a hurricane. Getting to the present, however, proved to have its own set of unique challenges. It was as if one was walking a tightrope at the cusp of Niagara Falls, one false step and you would slip into the future and be lost forever. Opposite forces of nature and physics met at this point in time and neither seemed particularly forgiving.

Alexi clung to John's shoulders as he used a cerulean light to return to the point in time they had fled, their present. Several times Alexi left out a shriek as she thought she was losing her grip on John but each time he pulled her closer. At last they spun into the very chairs from which they had left wearing the very same blood speckled clothes. After the chairs stopped spinning they came to a rest within the familiar sight of the New York City coffee shop. John sat smiling with a fresh cup of coffee in his hand while Alexi's coffee was spreading itself on the ground beneath the table Gottfried had shattered.

Alexi's heart was pounding as the chair she occupied spun into place next to John. John was happy to see there was no sign of Gottfried nor his men. People stood like statues around them as time was frozen as it had been when they departed. John seemed to be waiting for something and then off in the distance, echoing down the cavernous City came the distinctive call of the Raven. John let out a sigh, clicked his fingers and the table popped back together and even Alexi's coffee reconstituted itself in her hand, steaming hot.

"Welcome back to the present Alexi," said John matter-of-factly. "Sorry it was so traumatic, we were gone a long time and we had so much space in time to cover."

Alexi still had little understanding of time travel, but she could tell John was greatly relieved. To Alexi, it felt like years and years since she had last seen this café. She was not the same frightened teenager she'd been when she left this spot. Yet from what she could understand about time, her life would resume from the point in time at which she had left. Yet, she was so different. She had been transformed, how could life just start again from when she left?

She looked down at her mended clothes and the uncomfortable boots that John had bought her. She called upon the Way and using its red light transformed her clothes into more stylish clothes along with comfortable boots. As she wiggled her toes, she couldn't help but start to laugh and once she started she couldn't stop. She could barely get out the words, "What's the plan?"

As she laughed, John started to laugh as well. He clicked his fingers yet again and the people around them started to move in time once again. What these unfrozen people woke up to was a young man and a beautiful stylishly dressed younger woman laughing hilariously at something only they shared. However, as people walked by they all went their separate ways chuckling as well and feeling good about life. A bit of the lavender haze of the Way that seemed to hang lazily around Alexi rode gently among them.

Alexi was about to get out of her chair when John lightly touched her arm to hold her in place, motioning her to stay seated. She was a bit worried until she saw John had only been waiting for Matthew. He came around the corner with a huge grin appearing from beneath his red beard. He was appropriately dressed and wearing a magnificent smile.

As Matthew came up to them and greeted them both with hugs and pats on the back, he said, "I heard you both laughing from a block away. But, I for one never want to see this bloody café again."

His comment ignited another round of laughter and whole hearted agreement. The three of them sprinted from the café across the avenue toward Central Park. High overhead the Raven cawed and floated lazily in the bright cool sunlight of a late January day.

Before even getting across the street, Matthew gaped, "that's all she got for killing that troll was a mole. Why if I'd known that's all one gets for killing a wastrel like that I'd of killed him a hundred years ago." He smiled and added nodding toward Alexi, "Actually, it's quite becoming."

All three laughed and the sound attracted stares from other folks walking in the park on what was to them just an ordinary clear brisk January day. To the casual observer, they were just three college students enjoying their free time together. Alexi seemed to draw an occasional stare as an eye seemed to linger a bit longer on her. John realized it would have to be something she got used to from now on as the Way had marked her as special.

"I take it everything ended well at Woolsthorpe?" asked John.

"Aye, they all passed by the following morning. All in all it was very sad. I had hoped at least one of the lads would have repented. Gottfried nor the girl ever reappeared." Matthew said with finality. "We dug a mass grave using the Way and gave them all a decent burial, more than they deserved. I recognized most of them from my time here in New York. They were horrible men." John gave Matthew a confirming nod.

"It was hard leaving all the guys behind. I'm just starting to realize how much I miss them. Perhaps when this is all over the three of us can go back for a wee visit." said Matthew.

The gaiety of the moment seemed to pass, perhaps the reality of what was lost and all that remained yet to do set in upon them. Moments ago, their giddiness had been the result of recognizing all that they had been able to overcome. The seemingly impossible odds of just staying alive. But once Matthew called attention to the friends lost to them, the harshness of this reality struck John. Matthew saw the shadow come across John's face and a look of sympathy from Alexi. 'Did'ja see her John," asked Matthew realizing John was not thinking only of Hooke, Wren, Halley, Whiston and Cotes.

"Aye," said John. "When this is all over. We can go back for a visit." He let out a long sigh, "so let's finish it once and for all!"

"I do have a bit of news to share with you both. It's about Remy," said Matthew in a somber tone.

Alexi seized Matthew's arm, "He didn't survive did he?"

"Well, that's an interesting question. We'll need John to take a look at the creature. Wren and Hooke thought he was dead. Halley thought him alive, but barely. I really couldn't tell, but I was afraid to leave him behind to muck up our past or present. So when I came back, I brought him along," said Matthew.

"Where is he?" asked John as Alexi gave one last shudder.

Matthew smiled, "I thought it only fitting. I mounted him on a building at 214 West 29th street. He'll fit right in with the rest of the gargoyles on display there. Of course, I covered up the gold in a sort of stone and mildew. The Raven says he knows a few pigeons that hang out there and they'll be pleased to keep an eye on him."

"I'll have to take a look at him," said John. "In the meantime, I couldn't think of a more appropriate place." He patted Matthew on the shoulder and they continued walking in the present something they had not done together for forty years.

The first order of business was to find a place to call home. Matthew and the Raven were all for moving to another city if not another continent. John agreed wholeheartedly, but pointed out that they were the pursuers now. Gottfried needed medical attention and there was probably no better place to get it than New York City. Perhaps by watching the hospitals they could chase down their quarry.

The two men petitioned Alexi to identify the best Hotel in the town, ideally a penthouse that would provide the Raven easy access. They had been living on the edge for so long they wanted some place elegant. Once assuring her that cost was not an issue, when you can turn pebbles into gold you have no shortage of funds, they settled on staying at the Gotham suite at the Four Seasons. It overlooked the entire island of Manhattan and was close to Central Park. With amenities it ran a little less than fifty thousand dollars a day. The nice part was it came with a Bosendorfer grand piano and a complimentary Rolls-Royce.

Matthew's stash of funds and credit cards allowed them easy access to local currencies. As for clothes, the luggage they carried in with them through the Four Seasons' lobby was all for show and empty. They designed their clothes daily with the aid of the Way. Alexi found out that she had a particular flair that went beyond the jeans she grew up in. She was forever playing with whatever John and Matthew designed and kept changing what they wore sometimes as they walked out the door of their apartment.

John used the rose colored light of the Way to punch an invisible self-sealing hole into the window of the penthouse. The Raven was able to come and go as he pleased. The Raven, of course, was a big part of their new plan.

Before going to bed their first night back, despite everything that had happened that day, John and Matthew were able to construct from their memory three dimensional images of all the people they were looking for, including Gottfried and Bertha. Of course, there may be additional members of Gottfried's crew John explained to Alexi, but he felt confident with the images they were able to provide the Raven and his friends they should be able to track Gottfried down quickly if he was in the city.

The next morning Alexi was all for going and telling Professor Horowitz she was safe and he could go back to his teaching. John agreed Alexi should call him and tell the Professor she was safe, but that it would be best he remain hidden until Gottfried was finally taken out of the picture. Remember from the Professor's standpoint, he just saw you brutally beaten and rescued just three days ago. You might have a hard time explaining to him why you look so good. Alexi could only blush at the compliment and acknowledge John's logic.

On their second night back John and Matthew agreed to live dangerously and allow Alexi to select their evening meal. She was so excited to not be eating ten varieties of meat and chose sushi, curry, shrimp fried rice, pizza and nachos. After a bit of friendly debate, Matthew and John added beef tenderloin to the menu from room service.

"So, what's the plan?" asked Alexi as they each cracked open a fortune cookie.

Alexi saw Matthew look at John and give him a nod which seemed to say you tell her.

John cleared his throat, "Alexi, you've got to understand Gottfried is still very dangerous. The fact that the Raven's army has not found any of them these past forty-eight hours means Gottfried is still in control. Matthew and I both feel you would be much safer..."

Alexi cut him off, she had never envisioned that she would not be part of the team to see this through. "Look, I know I'm a novice in all this, but we're a team. I can look after myself and help cover your back." Her eyes were on fire. She was hurt, they would even think to leave her behind. After all, she was the one who had got rid of Remy.

"Now lassie," began Matthew sympathetically.

"Don't give me none of that now lassie crap," said Alexi defiantly. "I want to help!"

"It's too dangerous Alexi, it would be better..." started John.

But Alexi cut him off, "If I hid in the attic." Then throwing caution aside, she said, "If I sailed to Europe?" As soon as she said it, Alexi knew she'd gone too far.

Matthew winced while John's jaw firmed and he said, "Alright, I guess you earned it with all you been through and the reality is you'll be in danger no matter where we try and hide you. You can stay with us."

While she had won the argument, she felt terrible that she may have hurt John, who wiped his face with a napkin and left to go for a walk with the Raven.

As the door closed, Matthew left out a grunt and read his fortune out loud, "Beware the red headed woman." Matthew eyed Alexi dubiously and said, "See' n how your blonde I guess it's not you I have to be worried about."

Alexi smiled weakly and said, "Should I go after him. I didn't mean, how it came out."

"Nah, he'll be fine. However, well, it's really quite odd. You see lassie a dinner conversation very similar to this took place over a hundred years ago. I was not there, Wren, Hooke, John and Alexandra were the participants back then. Wren told me about it after the fact. Admittedly, it was over a different selection of food," he paused and tossed his fortune on the table and said sadly his voice breaking, "And it ended terribly, terribly," sighed Matthew forlornly.

Alexi sat back in the huge maroon leather winged back chair. "Can you tell me about it?" she asked, pulling her feet up on the chair beneath her. A look out the penthouse windows showed the skies were threatening a winter storm. The fire in the fireplace was offering up a warm glow throughout the room. Such a contrast to all they had been through, this seemed normal it was the point in time she belonged.

"Well, it's kind of a twisted tale," he paused to regain his composure. "At the time, John and I, along with Hooke, Halley and Wren were very concerned with the impending collapse of the Ottoman as well as the Austrian-Hungary empires. There was a lot taking place in the late nineteenth and early part of the twentieth century. Nature hates a vacuum and Gottfried was stirring up the Serbs, Greeks and Bulgarians by using the Prussian Junkers as his personal army. We thought at the time he was going to try and create his own empire in the Balkans. However, he had other plans and he convinced the new Kaiser, Wilhelm II, to relieve Gottfried's former student, Otto Von Bismarck, of his duties as Chancellor. Of course, what Gottfried was doing was laying the groundwork for Germany to subjugate France. We didn't know at the time, but all of his maneuvering was to lead directly into the First World War. So, as you can imagine they were very dangerous times. Yet, we had no idea how bad they were to become."

"It was about that time, a distant cousin of mine a Robert Falcon Scott, we called him the Falcon, wanted me to join him in the challenge to race to the South Pole and put a claim on Antarctica for the British Empire. He raised the funds to try and become the first man to set foot on the South Pole. Formally, it was the British Antarctica Expedition but was referred to as the Terra Nova Expedition. The gist of it was they were racing a Norwegian expedition led by Roald Amundsen. John and the rest of the crew thought it a great contest, but pointed out that there were more important matters to deal with in the Balkans. They also thought it would be unfair to use the Way in the competition and encouraged me to decline the offer."

"At the time, I reluctantly agreed to stay behind and help them in the Balkans. But about a year after the Falcon's team left, we heard they were having tremendous difficulties. I finally talked John into letting me go by myself and I left towards the end of 1911 with additional supplies. I thought I'd be a great asset and decided early on to only use the Way to save lives. Ah, but lassie, Antarctica is a barren and blighted land. And whether it's so because there are so few people in need of the Way in Antarctica or the cold and angle of the sun affects its disposition, for me the Way was impossible to call upon. As I said it's a forsaken land."

"Anyhow, I finally caught up with the Falcon as he was to make his final push to the pole. We actually got there, but we wound up being a few weeks behind Amundsen who had beaten us. In defeat, knowing we lost we turned to make our way back to the base camp only to run into terrible weather. Temperatures dropped from forty to sixty below. After several weeks, we'd gotten to a point just eleven miles from the base camp but could go no further. I laid my head down next to me dead cousin the Falcon and shut my eyes to die."

There was a long pause in Matthew's story, "The next thing I know, John was kneeling down by my side praying over me with the soft pink and lavender lights of the Way warming and mending my frostbitten extremities. While I couldn't call upon the Way, though I had tried repeatedly, John was able to bring it forth. He was too late to save anybody else on the expedition. The other eight men who I had left with on the final push to the pole all perished."

"It turns out John had a premonition that I was in dire need. He used the violet light of the Way to find me and ultimately put me back together," Matthew finished softly with a far off look in his eyes.

The room fell silent as Alexi tried to pull it all together, "And that's why you dedicated yourself to his release these last forty years," suggested Alexi softly.

"There's more lassie," said Matthew in a whisper. "Aye, I owe John my life, many times over. But in coming to Antarctica in April of 1912, he insisted Alexandra head to America for her own safety. He put her on the safest ship he could find. She wanted desperately to come with John and help him save me. But he refused, he felt the terrible weather would be too much for her. She was of a more delicate nature than you are lassie. So while John was busy saving me," tears were falling unapologetically into Matthew's red beard. "While John was distracted in saving me that April 14th, 1912, he lost Alexandra on the Titanic."

The next morning found the atmosphere in the palatial penthouse to be a bit more subdued and more businesslike. Even the Raven seemed a bit anxious that his team of over a thousand flying spies had failed him for the first time.

'Ach," exclaimed Matthew, "We dunno even if he stayed in the city. The only reason they were headquartered here in the first place was to keep you ensnared John."

They were sitting around a table full of maps of the city. Alexi had circled in red where each of the city's sixty-plus-hospitals were located. The Raven was nodding at each one verifying that they were all under constant observation.

"First, he'll have to undergo some procedure to cleanse his blood," said Alexi for the umpteenth time.

"I think it's safe to say that has already been done. But he must be weakened and, if not scared, very paranoid," said Matthew.

"Why scared?" asked Alexi.

"No tyrant ever feels safe having to rely upon the people they terrorize," said Matthew matter-of-factly.

"Matthew's right," said John as he looked over the maps. "He'll have to look outside his organization for the treatment first because he doesn't trust anyone and secondly, his access to the healing colors of the Way are unavailable to him. So the first thing he'll have done was to check into a private hospital. Where despite the unusual nature of his illness, he'll be able to buy them off and keep it hidden from the authorities. So, assuming him and Bertha are cured of the plague, sometime early next week he'll be looking for the best ophthalmologist to treat his eyes."

"I understand about the plague, but why his eyes? I thought you said he would regain his sight?" asked Alexi.

"Yes, but his eyesight is what provides his contact with the shadows. Unlike the whole realm of colors in the Way that we see, Gottfried needs near perfect vision to discern the subtle differences in the shadows," said John.

"So he's powerless?" asked Alexi.

"Well, lets' say weaker, but his paranoia will make him more dangerous. He'll be more likely to strike out at the least provocation," said John.

"Aye, we sent a shock wave into that soulless bastard's heart," added Matthew.

Alexi looked at the map and smiled as she tapped at a location with her pen. "Then we have him!" exclaimed Alexi.

"Sorry," said John.

"The Presbyterian Hospital at Columbia University is supposed to have the best Ophthalmology Department in the world. I remember hearing about an award they won while I was on campus, before all this began," said Alexi.

John and Matthew smiled, looking at the map. Even the Raven seemed to perk up at the news. Alexi stroked the bird's neck and back as it looked at the map. She had not been able to communicate directly with the Raven, but ever since John had told her Alexandra had been able to see what the Raven saw while in flight she was doing her best to befriend him. It seemed to be a mutually acceptable relationship as the Raven had begun to bring her back little baubles from his many flights. Including a huge diamond studded earring which she now wore in her right earlobe. It turned out to be a perfect prism as colors danced off it continuously. She was hesitant to ask how the Raven had procured it.

"We'll, have the Raven and his pals stake out the hospital," said Alexi excitedly. "They'll notify us when he shows up and we end this once and for all."

Matthew nodded and then added, "Yea, we should also ask the Raven's friends to be on the lookout for any concentration of the shadows. There are going to be a lot of angry and jumpy dark wizards about town. We'll have to round them up as well."

John was quiet for a while and then said, "Perhaps there's a better way."

chapter 17

THADDEUS

"How did you get such a terrible burn?" asked Dr. Thaddeus Jensen. The doctor was in his late-thirties, slim and of average height with a slightly receding hair line. He was one of the most celebrated physicians at the Columbia University Ophthalmology Center. The Doctor peered at the computerized image of his patient's scarred retina as with one experienced hand, he manipulated the electronic microscope behind his back.

"What does it matter?" asked his patient rudely with a deep German accent. "Can you use your lasers to remove the scars?"

Dr. Jensen was aware that his patient had just donated over a million dollars to the hospital building fund. The hospital's chairman had personally called him and all but demanded he see Herr Leibniz that very morning. It was highly unusual to say the least. And now this man with badly damaged eyes was treating him as if he was his servant. The Doctor wasn't used to being ordered about nor was he happy having to put off his other patients, but he learned long ago that ultimately, hospital politics and money could interfere and take precedence over his daily schedule.

"Having some knowledge of the cause will certainly affect my recommendation," said the Doctor calmly.

"Perhaps we should show him how you got those scars boss," suggested one of the patient's bodyguards. There were two bodyguards and they were dressed in suits more expensive than the Doctor himself could afford. What made them particularly frightening were the horrible scars that were prominently displayed across their faces. At first the Doctor thought they were perverse tattoos, but they seemed to be actually seeping. He could tell they were of the lowest class of street scum. Further, despite his best efforts to hide their effect on him, they knew he was scared of them. The physician had known such bullies in his youth, he'd been relentlessly picked on because his intelligence had caused him to be the target of jealousy. He thought he had left all that behind him. Now he realized the bullies of his youth just age to become bullies later in life. They thrive on exploiting fear and they enjoy it.

The Doctor knew he could call for security, but this was such a strange case with such an odd set of circumstances. He didn't want to escalate the encounter and see people get hurt. "Perhaps, you would be more comfortable with one of my colleagues," questioned the doctor knowing that it was probably useless.

"Karl, shut your mouth," said the patient, "you two step outside and watch the halls." The man called Karl glared at the doctor as he and his shadow left the room.

Despite the two guards leaving the office the tension in the small room did not subside. "It's difficult to get good protection, these days," declared Herr Leibniz. "Look Doc, I just need you to remove the scar tissue. Trust me the less you know the better."

"Herr Leibniz, you came here today to ask my opinion on how best to restore your eyesight. Your retinas have both been severely damaged. It's almost as if you looked directly into the sun."

"Ya, something like that," said Gottfried.

"I can prescribe some steroid drops that will grant you some immediate relief and we can schedule you for surgery next month," suggested the physician.

"Nein, tomorrow," said the heavily accented voice.

The Doctor gasped at his patient, "The drops will take at least thirty days to work. In the end you may not even need surgery. In any case, I dare not operate now. Let me rephrase that, no one should operate, before the muscle tissues are less inflamed. I've no means of knowing how they appeared before the accident but..."

The patient grabbed the doctor by his white cloak and forced him to look into his dilated eyes, "If you're lying to me Herr Doctor you'll not see the light of tomorrow's sun. If my enemies have gotten to you, let me assure you they can't protect you."

"See here, I've had just about enough of your intimidation. I suggest you go somewhere else." said the doctor regaining some courage. He stood up and brushed off his white medical jacket at the point Gottfried had grabbed it. He went to reach for the buzzer on his desk that security had installed the year before. Never in his wildest imagination had he ever envisioned himself having to use it.

The patient grabbed the doctor's white lapel and somehow prevented him from extending his right arm, "Nein, you'll do fine, but I need the operation tomorrow not a week from now."

"Look, I can't guarantee success if you undergo surgery without at least trying to let the swelling in your eyes go down first. Your eyes have been very badly damaged and they need some time. Please, if you don't believe me, get a second opinion," the Doctor was sweating and he was as scared as he'd been on the playground as a child.

"Give me the drops and schedule the operation for the day after tomorrow. I'm a fast healer!" declared Herr Leibniz with a terrible snarl.

"Look," the Doctor was about to object one last time and state that under no condition would he perform the surgery when he felt something cold and vicious grip his groin. He tried to scream, but something slimy and cold simultaneously entered his mouth and prevented any noise from forthcoming. He fell to his knees with tears streaming down his face from the excruciating pain.

"Schedule the surgery for the day after tomorrow at nine in the morning. If I find out you've been working with my enemies. Well, you haven't even felt a small amount of the pain I'm capable of inflicting," said Gottfried. The patient rose from his chair, threw the small paper bib aside that had been clipped to his chest and stepped over the Doctor's prostrate body and walked out of the office.

As the Doctor lay on the floor still trying to scream a lavender mist came flowing out of the air vent. When it reached the Doctor his pain eased immediately and his air passages were cleared from the black slime he couldn't even see. A few seconds later, John, Matthew and Alexi spun softly from the office's ventilation system back to their penthouse.

"Why threaten the Doctor you hope will heal you?' asked Alexi in disbelief at what she had just seen.

"Gottfried's scared," said Matthew. "He's scared we'll find him and he's scared his bodyguards will find out his powers have been tremendously weakened. As we saw back at Woolsthorpe, his men have very limited powers, but they have been given access to the shadows and together they could overthrow their master in his weakened condition. Gottfried has always been afraid anyone he trains will only try to topple him. He could always rely on Remy in the past to keep order in the ranks, now he's even lost him."

"I understand his paranoia, but still to threaten the man he expects to save his eyesight hardly seems logical," said Alexi.

"When Doctor Jensen sees Gottfried the day after tomorrow Gottfried will be as courteous and kind as the day is long. He'll be as kind as the Doctor's best friend. The Doctor will be so relieved he'll perform superbly," stated Matthew.

"And then, he'll kill the Doctor and everyone in that wing," added John. "That's why we couldn't risk taking Gottfried today. He and his men would've blown up the entire block. We need to take him alone, away from people and before his eyesight can be repaired. So we need a plan that will capture Gottfried once and for all and save that entire medical staff."

Alexi looked concerned, "Won't it be dangerous!"

"Of course, lassie" said Matthew with a twinkling, "All our plans are dangerous."

chapter 18

TANGO

"Who's she?" asked Herr Leibniz immediately upon entering Doctor Jensen's office on the morning scheduled for his surgery.

"My surgical assistant, she'll be helping me with your operation," stated a very nervous Dr. Jensen. He'd never experienced such pain as that inflicted upon him the day before by Gottfried. His first inclination was to run, far and fast, but that technique had failed him in his early days. Only when he had stood up to his playground antagonists had he been able to rid himself of their persecution and his fear. So when he met three extraordinary people, one of whom was the most beautiful woman he had ever laid eyes upon, he agreed to help. He did not require much convincing that his patient was an extraordinarily evil person. Nor that he needed to be stopped. However, when they told him their plan he required quite a bit of encouragement that it had even the slightest chance in hell of working.

The fact that Jensen was nervous was a good thing thought Alexi who was disguised, without the use of the Way, as Dr. Jensen's assistant. If Gottfried thought the Doctor wasn't afraid of him, he would have recognized something was amiss. She felt she could display her nervousness as well. Gottfried would expect the Doctor to have warned his brunette assistant with brown contacts set in her eyes with huge pink glasses that the patient was quite truculent. It also helped that the last time Gottfried had seen Alexi, she was a hysterical emotionally wrought recovering addict.

"Von wo sie sind schon?" asked Gottfried with a smile in German. (Where are you from beautiful?)

Not falling for the bait Alexi said, "Pardon?"

"Never mind," said Gottfried with a wave of his hand satisfied that the nurse knew no German. Gottfried had remembered that Bertha had told him the girl spoke fluent German. Always wary Gottfried thought it best to check. Nevertheless, after his demonstration of power the day before he had no doubt the Doctor would perform marvelously and would be too afraid to seek any assistance. "Let's get on with the procedure."

"Of course, of course, we both want a quick and successful operation. You'll make a matching donation to the hospital?" asked the Doctor playing his part.

"Ja, Ja," hissed the patient. I may even let you and your pretty nurse live thought Gottfried.

"It would be best," began the Doctor nervously, "if your three bodyguards would wait outside."

Alexi was worried that Gottfried would balk at this request. It wasn't an essential part of their plan, but it would make things easier.

Surprisingly Gottfried didn't hesitate so confident was he that he had scared the Doctor near to death. He gave the slightest nod to his three men and they went out into the reception area.

Alexi assisted the patient into the chair and as Dr. Jensen had instructed her, after she attached the paper bib, she put two drops in each of the patient's eyes. These were no ordinary drops, they would cause extreme dilation and greatly handicap Gottfried's already weakened eyesight. Alexi made certain that the drops were in both eyes and then waited for the drops to take affect before she went to apply a layer of gauze and bandages to Gottfried's right eye. As Alexi put the last piece of gauze in place she allowed the small finger of her right hand to slightly touch Gottfried's left temple.

The reaction was spontaneous and violent, "What's this betrügerei (*trickery*)," shrieked Gottfried. Alexi's slightest touch of Gottfried's temple had sent the full array of the Way's brightest colors into Gottfried's eyes. He'd never seen such an array of lights and power in his life. He was truly terrified.

He grabbed Alexi's right wrist and bent it back with such force it nearly snapped and Alexi left out a shriek of pain. "Karl, Karl get in here," he cried.

"Let her go," yelled Dr. Jensen quickly coming over to Alexi's aid.

Alexi wanted to shield the Doctor and tell him to stick to the plan, but it was too late. Gottfried, despite his very limited vision, summoned the shadows and with a swipe of his arm flung the Doctor and Alexi against the wall. "Karl, Karl," screamed Gottfried.

As Karl came rushing in to see what the problem was Alexi summoned the blue-gray light of the Way, and spun out of Gottfried's grasp. It was as if he was attempting to hold onto water vapor. As she spun, she was able to grasp the twitching foot of Dr. Jensen with her left hand and the two of them disappeared with a pop.

Had it not been for Karl's flirting with a cute nurse down the hall and the extraordinarily strong eye drops that Alexi had already placed in Gottfried's eyes Alexi and the Doctor may not have made their escape.

Gottfried despite his injury was still a very strong, paranoid and now very angry dark wizard.

Their escape and Karl's delay cost Karl his eyesight and then his life. As he sprang into the room Karl appeared to trip into the laser which by coincidence turned itself on and directed its beam of light into the former bodyguard's unprotected eyes. As the laser scrawled across Karl's face it eliminated his eyesight, well actually his eyes, forever.

Gottfried's rage was not so easily satiated. As he left the office the entire room exploded onto the street below. Karl's screams still resounded off the walls as Gottfried turned upon the spot he was standing and disappeared. His rage and adrenaline had made up for his limited sight. A sight so affected by the drops that he was unable to see the violet light of the Way that protected everyone but Karl from being killed in the explosion.

It was late the following day before Gottfried had calmed down. He and his remaining nine men plus Bertha were held up in a warehouse near wharf ten in Manhattan. There were scores and scores of dead birds around the outside of the building. Something that had all the neighbors up in alarm, in fear, that there had been some kind of chemical spill or gas leak in the area that remained unchecked.

"Where, where, where could she be? You're sure you've seen no traces of them? Not even that fool Doctor?" he had finally stopped screaming and was now very focused. His eyes had returned to their state before the botched surgery. "Have you used the shadows' ability to trace? Was it done properly, it has never failed before."

"They've simply van…vanished," stammered his new chief lieutenant Sebastian.

"They can't have just evaporated!" declared Bertha, who with the rescue of her boss at Woolsthorpe from sure death had risen to a very prominent position in the organization. Of course, Bertha had recently told Gottfried that Karl had insinuated that she should have left Gottfried to his own resources in England which was the real reason Karl had been eliminated. Of course, Karl had never said any such thing.

"More importantly, why place that fool of a girl in a position of such extreme danger. I had planned to kill them all once my operation was completed. Surely John would have expected as much. So, why place that fool of a girl to assist the good Doctor? Why not Matthew or John himself in disguise? If she hadn't accidentally touched my temple they probably would have burned out my eyes?" Gottfried kept asking himself these questions over and over. His power in the shadows was extraordinarily developed as it had taken centuries of training to explore much of the shadow's infinite powers. However, it was this power combined with his extraordinary intelligence that made him as dangerous as he had become.

"Why the girl? Why such an inexperienced wench? In Woolsthorpe they hadn't even used her in the stables. They attempted to protect her. Did you ever find out what happened to Remy?" He directed his question to Bertha.

"No, my master," said Bertha. "Why we still expect him, as you well know, at any moment."

Gottfried expected less and less that Remy had survived. It turned out to be a good thing for him that John and the rest of his damn fools had fled to see after the girl, but he doubted it could have helped Remy. However, to his point, if they all needed to run to see after the girl at Woolsthorpe why allow her such a dangerous role now? Obviously, they'd meant to use the Doctor to eliminate his sight, if she hadn't been nervous and given the plan away and touched his temple, he'd be all but dead. He could call her a fool, but he realized how close he'd come to being destroyed. This was the third time since John had escaped the bookstore that his life was clearly endangered. He had to be more careful, he reminded himself. These last forty years had made him and his entire organization go soft. In the end, thought Gottfried to himself, this cleansing will be for the betterment of his coven.

"Why the girl?" he mumbled out loud for the hundredth time.

"Maybe she was acting on her own," suggested a timid voice.

It was an angle Gottfried hadn't considered. "Erklären (*Explain*)," he hissed softly.

"Perhaps, she was trying to prove herself," suggested Bertha speaking a little more confidently. "When I posed as her chambermaid at Woolsthorpe, I listened as much as I could. The only thing she talked about was how kind and handsome she found John Newton. She was besotted. From what I've been able to gather, however, John Newton has always been in love with the German princess that went down with the Titanic. I think he was trying to teach this new girl how to use the Way while they walked the gardens, but I could never get close enough because of that dammed bird. What you described at the doctor's office would suggest she received some rudimentary training. But, if she is acting on her own now than perhaps they had a lover's quarrel."

Gottfried contemplated the suggestion and it was the only thing that made any sense. Of course, he hadn't considered the possibility of the girl's infatuation with Johnny. "Sebastian, were you with Remy when he killed the Princess?"

"Yes, my lord, you know I was there," responded, his lieutenant, "what's that have to do with..."

"Alles (*Everything*)!" Shouted Gottfried imagining that he and only he could have solved the riddle.

"Sebastian, go back in time to April 10, 1912 when the Titanic was preparing to sail. Go back and tell me if you notice anything different from the day the ship originally left the dock," said Gottfried in a steady voice trying to contain his excitement.

Sebastian spun on the spot. It was as if he hadn't been gone, but a moment before he spun back into the room.

"Das krähe (The *crow*)!" stated Gottfried before Sebastian could even talk.

"How did you know my Lord?" asked Sebastian. The other members of Gottfried's cadre were impressed. "The raven was circling the boat this time, but we never saw it when the ship originally sailed. I'm certain of it."

"So our lover boy couldn't wait to get back to his pretty wife. The new Doxy couldn't help but be jealous. She came back in a huff while those two yahoos, John and Matthew, try and figure out how to save Princess Alexandra and the other fifteen hundred passengers who died. The fools, if they do anything to change the past, they'll have to leave the present to me!"

"My lord," said a hesitant voice. "I mean after all these years. Is it possible?"

"You would've had to have seen the woman to understand. If not save her then at least spend time with her. He thinks he has me on the run. He thinks he has time to play. Remember, he was in cold storage the last forty years, and there is one thing I know about John Newton, his greatest weakness, he's an incurable romantic," Gottfried laughed hysterically certain he had it figured out.

"Sebastian, I want you to go back and take Jason and Pieter. You better take Johann as well. Alert Remy's former self that John and Matthew may show up after all and make sure all three of them go down with that damn ship!" screamed Gottfried.

"That doesn't leave you too much help my lord." Sebastian knew he had misspoke as soon as the words left his mouth. He was getting anxious that Bertha was gaining too much power. Fortunately for Sebastian at that time one of the scouts rushed in with news.

"We spotted the girl and the Doctor they got on a commercial flight to Buenos Aires," said the scout.

"Were they alone?" asked Gottfried. The scout, a person used by Gottfried despite the fact that he'd shown no power in the shadows, nodded affirmatively. At first Gottfried was a bit shocked that the girl had given up her limited use of the Way so quickly. She could easily have taken the Doctor with her wherever she wanted to go without taking an airplane and exposing herself. But this just supported his theory that she was on her own. She was on the run trying to protect her unwary accomplice, the good Doctor and she didn't want to leave a trace that would be left if she used the Way. "So she's on the run. Silly girl, silly, silly girl." he mused.

"She's not very bright," sneered Bertha knowing this was not true at all. The girl had been extremely clever at Woolsthorpe giving up nothing that Bertha could send back to Gottfried. However, she knew Gottfried would enjoy hearing a confirmation that the girl was a fool.

"Alright then our path seems clear. We go capture the girl and get rid of the good Doctor. Landis and Siegfried you're coming with me. We're going to tango," said Gottfried with a smile.

"But my lord," said a disappointed Bertha that she was not asked to go. "Shouldn't you get your surgery first?"

Gottfried was in too big of a rush to even take the comment as criticism, even as skepticism, "If we let the trail go cold we'll never catch the girl. Even with my somewhat limited sight I can manage a fool of a teenage girl. We catch her and we have John Newton, whether he goes down with the Titanic or comes back to the present. We hold the girl and in the end Johnny will come crawling to me on his knees!" cried Gottfried.

chapter 19

PERDITION

Aerolineas Airlines, the Argentine airline, offered the only non-stop flight from New York City to Buenos Aires, Argentina. Despite the fact that the flight had left hours ago, it was an eleven hour flight, Gottfried knew they had plenty of time before they needed to depart. Even if the girl used the Way to leave the flight before the plane landed they would know. The strategy going forward, as it stood, was quite simple, said Gottfried to himself, as he waited for the appropriate time for departure. We use the shadows to beat them to the Ministro Pisarini Airport in Buenos Aires. We seize them as they come off the plane, dispose of the Doctor and drag the girl back here and wait for Johnny. A simple plan, but just like in Woolsthorpe he was having a twinge of anxiety.

Perhaps he should have his eyes attended to by another doctor first. He would have to get the surgery in any case. His prospects for catching the girl, however, would never be better. He tried to tell himself the girl's escape from the doctor's office was because it caught him so unaware and the stupid drops had made his sight weaker than it is even now. Then there was the gnawing truth that even with perfect eyesight John had recently handed him some bitter defeats. He would never admit this to his group of followers, but the truth was John had outsmarted him. John was a more than worthy adversary and had proven so throughout the last three hundred years. He needed a bargaining chip, he needed the girl. Once he was in possession of the girl John would do anything he wanted including giving himself up. He realized the girl was the key.

It was very unnerving and a bit ironic thought Gottfried that the plane he now needed to intercept would be flying into Ministro Pisarini Airport. He was there in 1945 when they laid the cornerstone to the terminal. At the time, he and Remy had fled Germany with John and his whole gang in pursuit. Well, this time he was the pursuer, enough self-doubt, on to Argentina!

Gottfried, Landis and Siegfried arrived at the Argentine airport with plenty of time to spare. As planned they had merely pulled the dark violet light wave from the shadows, concentrated on the Airport and spun into Argentina. The extra time was used to make sure nothing was amiss. The three men waited discreetly just outside of Argentine customs watching as the passengers came off the airplane. They would use a simple time freezing spell, grab the runaways and be gone. Home in time for dinner smiled Gottfried to himself.

They were shortly upset, however, when it appeared the doctor and the girl had failed to come off the airplane. A few discreet inquiries led them to a stewardess who under the influence of the shadows said she remembered the couple as described on the flight. Yes, they seemed very nervous initially when they got on the flight, but seemed to relax after the flight departed. She was certain they'd gotten off the plane because the young lady asked where they would have to go in the terminal to catch their flight to Tierra del Fuego. Not many people chose to travel to Argentina's southernmost province.

Siegfried and Landis checked at the counter, and for a few hundred pesos they found out that only two American passengers on the flight from JFK had purchased tickets going on to the southern city of Rio Grande. Contrary to the inquiry, it was two elderly gentlemen and not a young woman and middle aged man.

"They must have been disguised as they got off the plane, my lord," suggested Landis.

"Of course they were disguised you idiot! You let them slip right past us! Did neither of you even consider to see if they were using the Way to disguise themselves? Clearly, I'm working with idiots," Gottfried could hardly contain his anger and things were not adding up. Why this senseless journey to the middle of nowhere?

Landis and Siegfried eyed each other knowingly. They dared not point out that it was Gottfried that had failed to notice the two cloaked in the Way. Landis and Siegfried had actually been ordered onto the plane to try and see why it was taking the two passengers so long to get off. Gottfried had been left standing at the gate and they had walked right past him and his impaired vision.

"What difference does it make? We'll wait for them in Rio let's go. With that, they spun to the Airport in Rio Grande, Argentina.

The flight to Rio Grande never arrived. After much haggling and excessive use of the shadow's mind numbing techniques Gottfried was told for some unfathomed reason the flight had been diverted at the last minute to Ushuaria the southernmost city in the world. By this time Gottfried was beside himself with rage while the two hapless men who had accompanied him realized they were lucky still to be alive. They had almost fled, but realized there was no place to run. Their fortunes had been tied to Gottfried Leibniz long ago.

Gottfried was tired of being outfoxed by this teenage girl and his rage could hardly be contained when they discovered in Ushuaria that a nervous middle aged man, who fit the description of the ophthalmologist and a strikingly beautiful blonde girl had immediately booked passage and departed on an expedition to the South Pole. Gottfried hated Antarctica, everything was too bright. The shadows were hard to reach. Nonetheless, they put themselves in the mindset to go after them. The only problem was that the tour company that the two had apparently used was so small there was no one left to question, or maim. Everyone was on the boat south to the continent and if the girl didn't use the Way, even for disguise, once she got off the boat she would be near impossible to find.

By now the three pursuers were very tired, very exasperated and all but jumping down each other's throat. While Landis and Siegfried were still wary of Gottfried's great powers they had little doubt that the girl had played him for a fool. She had a plan and it was working all too well. They had little doubt that the young woman would indeed get away if she didn't use the Way and leave a traceable event.

"My lord, we require more help," suggested Landis.

"Nonsense, you think I can't track down a teenage girl. See here, they had to arrive at one of three ports and we've checked the other two. You go over to that official, use the black mind meld I taught you at that last forsaken place and find out which way they went," said an irritable Gottfried.

It took Landis about fifteen minutes as the technique he was told to use was tricky. While it did provide the absolute truth from the victim, it was a bit clumsy as once used it left the person debilitated for days. Its use also left Landis a noticeable and painful limp.

Landis returned and told Gottfried, "They headed due south to the pole, my Lord. They had snowmobiles waiting for them there upon arrival. The man was struck by the girl's..."

"Yes, yes", interrupted Gottfried exasperated, "the girl's beauty."

"My lord, there are no more snowmobiles. There were only two in working order and they were the ones the girl and the doctor took," said a tired and dreary Landis.

Gottfried had enough and shouted, "My god man go and get us a helicopter!"

"A storm is coming in, my lord, no one will fly us." Sebastian practically screamed.

Gottfried went over to counter where the helicopters normally were rented with a pilot and within two minutes he was walking back with a set of keys. "Come on, let's get this over with."

The helicopter was an older model, but it mattered little to Gottfried. He just wanted a platform from which the three men could project the shadows to search for the two fugitives who would at last be captured. He felt confident that despite the wild goose chase they would have little difficulty in finding the two fleeing life forms in this barren wilderness.

As they flew along the barren landscape assured that they would soon capture the girl, he thought of the need to kill both of the men that currently accompanied him before they headed back to New York. It would do no good to have the facts about this trip spread around to the rest of his followers. While he admitted to himself that his ranks were getting a bit thin these two were obviously incompetent. They needed to be disposed of as soon as possible. Whatever was Remy thinking of keeping these two idiots?

They had flown through the night and daybreak was just easing itself over the barren landscape. By this time they were being held aloft by the shadows, the fuel long having been depleted several hours past just as the storm subsided. With the aid of the morning sun Landis called out, "There, my lord, up ahead, I see something."

"Me too!" shouted Siegfried.

"Where, I don't see anything," said Gottfried, who had been forced to wear sunglasses because of the bright light reflecting off the snow hurting his wounded eyes.

"Directly south, my lord, you can't miss it," said Landis.

"Penguins," said a disgusted Gottfried, "thousands of them."

"Yes, Yes, but also something much larger, my lord, a hut and two snowmobiles. I can even see some trace of the Way. It's a very weak use, but it's certainly the colors of the Way." Their journey had ended at last.

As the helicopter landed the three men crawled out of the helicopter and were immediately struck by how cold it was and the vast number of penguins that almost hid the snow beneath them. The three men drew on the shadows of the Way for warmth. Gottfried gestured for the two men to halt as they neared the shack. "You two get rid of these penguins!" said Gottfried.

"My lord, there must be ten thousand or more," said Landis astonished at the request.

"You heard me. Kill them all. I hate birds," said Gottfried, who expected the deed done once it was ordered. Gottfried attempted to call upon the shadows once more and was taken aback at how unresponsive they were to his call. Normally, they obeyed him without hesitation. The Antarctica affect combined with his damaged eyes and lack of sleep seemed to have combined to make it almost impossible to spark their interest. At last he was able to contact the shadows and have them seep into the hut. It was like listening to an AM station with a weak signal when you were used to the first row at the Vienna Symphony. Well, thought Gottfried as his two minions waded into the penguins, there's no turning back now. With a flourish Gottfried entered the hut as weak as he had been in two centuries, but he told himself it's only a teenage girl.

It was misty inside the hut as the heat pulled from the colors of the Way reacted with the cold air seeping in through the hut's cracks. It required Gottfried a moment to adjust, but as he did, he noticed, but one small robed and hooded figure kneeling with its back to the door and hence to Gottfried.

"Your little chase has ended Fraulein, your foolish game has come to an end. The Doctor, wherever he is, will be killed of course. Come along quietly and I'll make it quick for him otherwise he'll die in a pain you'll both share." The figure didn't move. In fact, it seemed to be praying. This fact infuriated Gottfried all the more and he strove over to rip his victim's hood off and make her face him.

Gottfried grabbed the hood and jerked his victim's head back in such a fashion so that he could look into what he anticipated to be eyes of terror. Instead of green eyes of horror, he beheld blue eyes shining in unabashed victory as John's disguise as Alexi slowly melted away. Gottfried's eye contact with John was short lived as he and the walls of the hut were blown away by a powerful wind. Gottfried, who had been blown backwards and was now on his back in a daze was having trouble gathering his senses. The loss of the walls, exposed him to the cold and bright cool sunlight.

It was with the elimination of the hut that the raven-disguised-as-a-penguin turned back to a raven and with a loud caw swept in at Gottfried's face and plucked the sunglasses off his eyes. Gottfried left out a scream of pain as the light reflecting off the snow struck his fragile retinas. His two lieutenants that had been instructed to kill the penguins and, by default, any raven-disguised-as-a-penguin stood frozen, completely paralyzed.

As Gottfried began to recover, he saw the kneeling figure, whom he had mistaken to be Alexi turn around to reveal himself as John Newton. Gottfried turned in shock and saw Matthew, Alexi and Doctor Jensen rise up from their disguises as penguins.

"How, why," stuttered a stunned Gottfried, "what's the meaning of this?"

"I just love it when a plan comes together'," said Matthew. The Raven happy to no longer be disguised as a penguin gave out a happy caw.

"You lured me here. Why not simply kill me in the doctor's office and be done with it?" he sneered.

"Ah well," said John. "Too many people could be hurt. We also needed to show the Way how serious you were about trying to kill Alexi and the Doctor. How determined at each decision point you were that you would follow them even here to the ends of the earth."

"What do you mean to do with me?" asked Gottfried defiantly. "Your Way won't let you kill me if I seek redemption." Gottfried thought he could tell by the twitch in John's jaw that it was the one thing John had never anticipated. "That's right Johnny boy!" Gottfried screamed. "I seek redemption and you have to give it to me! You can't kill me!"

The smile that John gave Gottfried caught him by surprise. "Of course, we always hoped you would choose such a path Herr Leibniz. That was the other reason for bringing you here," said John.

"Welcome to your new home Gottfried," said Matthew. 'I hope you like penguins."

"Of course, as you say you choose to seek redemption, so you of all people realize you have a great deal to be forgiven and will need a place of absolute solitude to pray. You should have few interruptions as you pray for forgiveness. You'll find you can't move more than twenty feet in any direction from this spot. You'll need what limited use of the shadows made available to you with your limited eyesight to provide you enough comfort for warmth and sustenance. Only when the colors of the Way accept that you've truly been redeemed will you be able to leave and even then it will be as a mortal without any access to the power of the shadows," said John.

Gottfried screamed and ran toward Alexi only to be thrown back as he hit an invisible wall. "No," he screamed and he rolled into a ball crying hysterically.

John turned to leave realizing he gathered little satisfaction in seeing his enemy of close to three centuries crying in a heap of self-pity. The man that had ordered the death of his wife and had in one way or another inflicted and was responsible for the deaths of millions was no more. The great dark lord was all but dead left to a fate that provided him one last chance. Nonetheless, John suspected he would fail to take advantage of this one last opportunity.

Gottfried, however, was actually quite happy to see John turn his back to him under the assumption he had won. With John's back to him and Matthew turning away to assist the Doctor, Gottfried rose up and called upon the force of the shadows to kill John Newton once and for all. What would a small disfigurement be compared to an isolated cell.

The only one watching the pitiful display to the end was Alexi and as she saw this monster reach out to kill the man she loved, she too called upon the Way and grasped the light that it readily offered up to her. It was, of course, the golden light and with a sweep of her hand, she turned the unrepentant German into a statue of gold as she had his secretary before him. Gottfried's cry of agony as his body slowly turned to solid gold was caught in the newly minted statue's look of confusion and self-pity as he realized what was happening.

Two of the three unfrozen men turned around in shock. John smiled to himself, knowing that the final possibility that his plan allowed for was actually coming to fruition. This portion of his plan, not shared with anyone else, had allowed for this eventuality, for Alexi to spontaneously offer up a more permanent solution to the evil that had wreaked havoc for all these centuries. John was relying upon his theory that the Way truly saw Alexi as its favorite. As such, the Way would not punish her severely for this last indiscretion. Especially after Gottfried had shown such determination to capture and maim if not kill her. As such, Gottfried Leibniz with a face of rage that made him look as disfigured as the gargoyles on 29th street was turned to solid gold. John told himself as he looked on the golden figure that he hoped Gottfried Leibniz would repose in perdition for eternity.

It was only after the spell was cast that all the men then turned to Alexi and looked at her in shock.

"What!" she cried.

John was the first to recover. He was stoic as he walked toward Alexi offering her a mirror he had manufactured out of the air.

"No," she screamed, "it's not fair. I had no choice," as tears streamed down her face.

Matthew came up from behind her chuckling, "Now lassie, red hair is nothing to be ashamed of."

"It's not just red hair," wailed Alexi flinging herself into John's arms to continue crying.

Matthew and the Doctor looked at John over Alexi's shoulder not able to see her face as she was crying into John's shoulder. For a moment they feared the worst when John looked out over the crying woman in his arms, smiling broadly, he mouthed the word "freckles."

chapter 20

ROCK & ROLL

"I can't believe it's finally over," said Matthew as he hugged his friend of over three hundred years. Matthew next dragged into his hug the red haired freckled Alexi. "We couldn't have done it without you lassie."

Alexi smiled and kissed him and then John on their cheeks. Her red hair a bit brighter than the Scot's. "Is it over?" asked Alexi.

They were standing at 214 West 29th street just a couple of blocks from Madison Square Garden in New York City. Snowflakes were just starting to fall with a purpose. They were admiring their handiwork of the night before which had seen them positioning a new gargoyle to face the one Matthew had added just a couple of weeks before. The two new statues now facing each other offered up to their counterpart an eternal face of primeval rage. A group of the Raven's pigeon friends was testing out their new roosts.

"Well, it's not over yet. While we did get Saul and Thaddeus back to work, we still have a few unrepentant servers of the shadows to apprehend. I wasn't surprised Landis and Siegfried gave up their attraction to the dark side given the trip of horror they just completed with Gottfried. It's nice to see someone actually acknowledge their poor decisions and seek the light," sighed John. "Still, once that power is activated in a soul, it's hard to turn off. I hope they make it."

"I was surprised the Way accepted their petition so quickly," said Alexi.

"Aye," said Matthew. "It's a shame that the Way stripped them of any access. We could use a few recruits."

John sighed once again, "The one that scares me the most is this Bertha."

Alexi gave a shudder, "Even for an eighteenth century maid she seemed a bit off, very dark. Frankly, she scares me too. She could be so nice at times, but it was a clever façade. She was so cold and calculating. I can still her laugh when she opened the door to the attic for Remy. It was pure evil."

"I think I found out a little about her," John began.

Matthew interrupted, "Ach, will you two give it a rest. However, evil she may be she ain't a hill of beans compared to Gottfried. And we promised the Raven as soon as the gargoyles were in place we'd be leaving New York City for good!"

John smiled and waited until Matthew and Alexi acknowledged him with a nod. He grabbed each by the hand and then in a blue-gray mist spun on the spot and disappeared. None of them cared if anyone in New York City saw them disappear. They had no intentions of ever returning.

A few days later, after what seemed like a non-stop buying spree to an enthusiastic and fully participating Alexi, they found themselves in the Caribbean once again anchored off the island of Exuma in the Bahamas. It was where they had gone on the offensive against Gottfried. The beginning of an adventure that literally and figuratively seemed to have taken place hundreds of years ago. Alexi was wearing a modest white one piece swimsuit with a huge fashionable powder blue straw-spun sun hat. She had rapidly found out that unlike her blonde body which loved the sunshine, her red headed freckled body abhorred it. She was still trying to get herself accustomed to the red hair. Matthew jovially told her that he always found the opposite sex loved red heads the best. John seemed a bit quiet about the subject only saying that the Way had remade her into a new and unique person.

At the moment the sky and the sea seemed to blend into the perfect crystal blue horizon. The yacht John had bought in Miami was more modern than the original *Principia* with which it shared the same name. Happily for Alexi, the new one had many more creature comforts including a deluxe master suite which she had all to herself. The boys had spared nothing in supplying her with all the latest fashions and every conceivable luxury. "The boys", was how Alexi had started referring to them. It was better than three hundred year old wizards she thought.

John and Matthew had slept almost all of the first two days that they were anchored off the island. It gave Alexi plenty of time to get acquainted with the sun and realize her skin's new limitations. This morning the boys well rested, had gone ashore promising to come back with a variety of fresh food. Alexi had smiled let them go and called on the Way, which in turn delivered into her outstretched palms a five pound red fish from right out of the ocean. She cleaned it and had it, broiling in the ship's galley when Matthew spun back onto the ship.

Matthew smiled at the aroma coming up from the galley. "Where's John?" asked Alexi. She rarely, if ever, saw the two of them apart anymore.

"Oh, he'll be along in a sec," said Matthew. "He feels he may have found the old wreck of the original *Principia*."

Matthew, who'd been diving with John dried himself off with a huge towel and then addressed Alexi. "Lassie," said Matthew as their eyes met.

Alexi sensed something was wrong, he seemed very serious, "What is it Matthew?" she asked with concern.

"Well, I just want you to know," Matthew paused. "What I mean is, I think of ye like my own daughter."

Alexi looked on somewhat bemused, but said nothing.

"You see I was looking out for you ever since you were a wee babe," said Matthew. "I'm mighty proud of the how ye turned out. Mighty proud… and the thing is if I'm not mistaken, well, I think I noticed you may have taken a wee bit of a romantic interest in John."

Alexi started to protest, but Matthew held up his hand to stop her. "Look, if I did have a daughter, well, I'd want that daughter to know that if she had any interest in John Newton," at this point Matthew found himself a bit tongue tied particularly since Alexi was smiling at him so brightly. "Well, what I mean to say is, why there is no better man in this here world than John Newton." Matthew was now blushing which made him appear even more red than usual.

"John is a great man," said Alexi agreeing whole heartedly and smiling more broadly.

"Exactly, but the thing of it is lassie," said Matthew now about to get to the nub of the matter, "His love for Alexandra has never died." There he had said it, but he knew however painful it was to Alexi, it had to be brought out in the open.

Alexi looked a bit taken aback, she liked where the conversation was headed before. Her hat afforded her some shelter from Matthew seeing the tear that had suddenly appeared out of nowhere. She turned away from Matthew and looked out to sea in the opposite direction.

"But, well," Matthew knew instinctively that this was not going as planned. The Raven flew down beside him and left out a soft caw of encouragement.

Matthew nodded at the Raven, "the thing is before John had been captured in that curse he had been spending more and more time with Alexandra, in the past."

"He could do that?" asked Alexi the tears running down her cheeks were now a bit harder to hide since she had to wipe them with her hand.

"Yes, but it was very difficult and it drained him of his ability to function in the present. I think it led directly to his capture. When you go back to the past, there's very little pain, very few surprises. You can get very comfortable in the past to the point that the two worlds conflict and it becomes harder and harder to discern reality. Plus, John had to make sure Alexandra knew nothing of her impending fate. You can imagine how near impossible that would be."

"I think John had reached the point that Isaac once warned us about. If you live in the past you can never move forward. That's why Isaac risked everything and leapt into the future. It's also why when we visit the past, we never manage to catch up with Isaac. He's moved on. John, however, wouldn't listen to reason. He wouldn't hear of living life without Alexandra. Me and the Raven needed a plan to set John free," Matthew added softly.

Alexi suddenly understood what Matthew was trying to tell her. She tried to catch her breath and stop her tears. Matthew was not trying to say John could never love her, in fact, it was the exact opposite.

"That's right," said Matthew sensing that Alexi understood. "John was to the point of staying behind, leaving the present. He realized that he couldn't save Alexandra and return here to us. The past would be changed, he and Alexandra would be on their own path in time. He would be lost forever." The Raven cawed in affirmation.

"When we cloned you lassie," said Matthew softly, "well, as we raised you..."

Alexi cut Matthew off, she turned to face him, tears still streaming down her face, "You said once that only John Newton could free himself from Gottfried and I realize now you were absolutely right. No one but John could have escaped from that café let alone take me with him. But you also once told me that I was conceived to free John. I thought you meant from the bookstore, but you meant I was to free him from his past." She buried her head in Matthew's massive shoulder crying tears of joy at last understanding that not only was there a future for her with John. Without her, John had no future.

Fortunately, John did not return from the old *Principia* to the new until Alexi had finished crying and both, she and Matthew, were able to get their dispositions back in order. While the three of them, Matthew, Alexi and the Raven were in a better frame of mind than just a short time before the mood at dinner was uncharacteristically somber.

Despite John lavishing compliments on Alexi for the meal and having provided some beautiful music, both Alexi and Matthew seemed a bit distant. "I know," said John. "Perhaps, it's time for a break. I mean a real break. How bout we go dancing." He eyed Matthew knowingly, "Let's say we go back to the time Catherine gave a ball for us at her summer palace. You remember, Matthew, when we first accompanied John Paul Jones to her court! Alexi would love the dancing. She wouldn't go ten minutes without a hundred men wanting to get on her dance card!"

It brought a smile to Matthew's face, "Or maybe to the celebration galas in Vienna after the battle of Waterloo. Do ya ever remember seeing such beautiful women?"

Despite the positive change in the atmosphere between the boys, Alexi looked on but didn't smile. "What's wrong?" asked John. "It'll be great. You'll get to see some of the guys from Woolsthorpe as well."

"True," said Alexi coyly. "But you've just seen them John. Lets' forget the past for a while and remain here in the present." Her voice became stronger, "I have a different plan. I'm taking you two boys to see some rock-and-roll. You don't know what you've been miss'n."

[Music: Made to love you by TobyMac] https://www.youtube.com/watch?v=cFJ5qCmvPkY

EPILOGUE

The storm that came in that night caught everyone in New York City by surprise. The forecasters had predicted clear skies, but an unusual squaw came in off the Atlantic and everyone heading to the ACC tournament at Madison Square Garden that did not come in by train was caught in a pouring rain. The cause of the storm could actually be found at 214 West 29th street. Up amongst two of the newer gargoyles sat Bertha Holtmeyer. In her present form she would have made an excellent addition to the other gargoyles except for the fact that she was alive. Although it would depend upon the definition of the word.

Bertha had suffered terrible retribution from the Way as she fought and killed off former members of her master's coven. She had tortured Siegfried and Landis unmercifully before she killed them. Between their screams of pain she had learned everything that had occurred on their fateful trip to Antarctica. Bertha and Bertha alone now stood as the heir and keeper of the once powerful Herr Gottfried Leibniz's coven. Her spine was twisted and her face deeply scarred. Her hair almost taking on a life of its own as it twisted and continually dripped beads of blood moved about with a will of its own.

Despite her disfigurement she considered herself quite fortunate and very happy. She had been tracking the whereabouts of John Newton when she saw him along with his two cohorts disappear a month ago directly in front of the building she now sat upon. Something seemed to call her from above and as she focused on the statuettes they seemed to call to her via the shadows. It was not difficult for her to make out the image of Remy, but she cried and cried when she discovered that her master was entombed here as well. "Oh, they'll pay, they'll pay for what they've done Master," she wept over and over as a pool of blood gathered around her shoes and the bodies of the dead pigeons at her feet.